Diablo – Days of Darkness

Gabi Adam

Diablo –
Days of Darkness

Copyright: © Gabi Adam 2008
The plot and the names of the characters are entirely fictional.
Original Title: DIABOLO - Tage der Finsternis
Cover photo: © Bob Langrish
Cover layout: Stabenfeldt A/S
Translated by Barclay House Publishing
Typeset by Roberta L. Melzl
Editor: Bobbie Chase
Printed in Germany, 2008

ISBN: 978-1-933343-83-9

Stabenfeldt, Inc.
457 North Main Street
Danbury, CT 06811
www.pony4kids.com

Available exclusively through PONY Book Club.

For all those who never give up – no matter what.

Chapter 1

"Uaaahhh ..." Fourteen-year-old Ricki Sulai lay in her bed, yawned loudly, and stretched herself into an upright position. The brilliant January sunrise streaming through the window illuminated every corner of her bedroom, making it impossible for her to go back to sleep even if she wanted to. And today, especially, she didn't want to.

What a beautiful day, she thought to herself. *And the best part of it is there's no school!* The annual High School Teachers' Refresher Seminar was being held at the state university. Ricki loved this bonus vacation. The teachers had to go to school while she and her friends could go riding.

How happy she was. Only yesterday her boyfriend, Kevin Thomas, had given her a quick hug and told her that he was crazy about her and couldn't imagine being without her. Dreamily, she recalled the image. She could still hear Kevin's voice in her head and she felt an overwhelming joy in her heart because of him.

Ricki sighed contentedly, but then she had to laugh.

5

Her girlfriends, Lillian Bates and Cathy Sutherland, who had witnessed Kevin's declaration of devotion, had just grinned at each other.

"Oh, brother," Cathy said as an aside to Lillian. "Can't you just see the two of them, an old married couple, sitting on a park bench holding hands and reminiscing about how wonderful it used to be when they were young and didn't have to worry about their dentures wobbling or their eyeglasses tangling when they kissed?"

"You've painted a charming picture, Cathy," Kevin said wryly. "But at least you have Ricki and me together as an 'old married couple.' How are you guys doing with your 'love lives'? What about you, Lillian? We haven't heard much about Josh lately. Are you two still dating?"

Lillian's face darkened. "Yeah," she said, drawing the word out, "but we're not getting along very well just now."

"What?" Cathy asked in surprise. "I thought you two were the original dream couple, after Ricki and Kevin, of course."

Lillian shrugged her shoulders. "Yeah, but he's always after me to start riding Western style and accompany him to all his riding shows. And that's impossible. Holli just isn't a Western-style horse, and I'm not about to trade him in for a quarter horse just to please Josh. Besides, I don't have the time to spend every weekend with him at horse shows. I've got school every weekday and homework every night, and I have to help out on the farm every once in a while. If I have any free time left, I'm going to spend it with Holli. After all, he has to have regular exercise and grooming, and I'm not going to leave him uncared-for and alone in his stall just so I can cheer while Josh and Cherish win another first prize."

Ricki nodded. "That's true, but Josh, being a rider, should understand that."

"Yeah, you'd think so, but I've got a feeling something else is going on here, and that his obsession with Western riding is just an excuse, a cover. He talks about Rebecca all the time, and she's been at the ranch practically every day for the past six weeks. Supposedly, she has a fabulous pinto mare, with excellent training, and she goes to all the shows as well. Josh just keeps raving about the horse and the girl, how they are so fantastically suited to each other, and real competition for him."

"Well, then, your Josh is just going to have to work a little harder in the future if he wants to beat her," Cathy said playfully. Lillian shook her head and exhaled deeply.

"*My* Josh!" she shouted. "I think that *my* Josh has a crush on Rebecca. You should see how his eyes light up when he talks about her."

"Oh, come on, Lillian, you're probably just imagining all this," Kevin said, trying to comfort his friend. "Josh isn't like that." However, the three teenagers looked sad.

"Believe me, it's not my imagination. It feels like he's distancing himself from me, and you know what? That really hurts!"

*

Ricki pulled back her blanket and swung her legs out of bed. Awkwardly, she tried to find her slippers with her feet.

Josh would be an idiot if he dumped Lillian, she thought.

7

He doesn't seem to realize what he could lose. Then she saw the image of Kevin before her, and the thought that he could like someone else better than Ricki made her stomach ache.

"That's nonsense!" Ricki shuffled into the bathroom where she splashed her face with ice-cold water. She gazed at her reflection in the mirror. What had Kevin said to her? That she had the most beautiful eyes in the world? Ricki smiled. At the moment, a fairly sleepy face was looking back at her; one that needed to wake up before it was ready for compliments.

While Ricki was getting dressed, she tried to remember what time the four friends had decided to get together. Was it one o'clock or two o'clock?

"Darn it, I can't remember anymore!" Ricki grabbed the hairbrush and tried to get her mane under control, but today her hair was going in all directions. She decided to take a scrunchy and make a ponytail. She knew that Kevin would take one look at her and frown, as usual deciding that she looked better with her hair down.

"Whatever!" With one last satisfied glance at her reflection in the mirror, she left the bathroom and tiptoed down the creaking stairs as quietly as possible. It was still early, and she didn't want to wake up anyone else in the family – especially not her little brother, Harry, who would definitely get on her nerves again, trying to get her to take him with her when she went riding.

In the mudroom she grabbed her quilted jacket from the hook, slipped into her old boots, and then closed the door quietly behind her. She ran over to the stable. She could already hear the familiar scratching of the pitchfork on the cement floor. Jake, the elderly stableman and groom, was already hard at work.

"Good morning!" On her way to Diablo, she called to him. She gave the old man, whom she and Harry had "adopted" as their grandfather, a quick kiss on the cheek. Then she wrapped her arms around her black horse's neck.

"Morning!" grumbled Jake and wiped his cheek. "You're in a good mood this morning! What did I do to earn a kiss from you?"

Ricki laughed. "Well, there's no one else here!" she grinned, and held up a treat for Diablo.

"How disappointing to find out that young girls kiss me only if no one else is available," he grinned back at her. Then he began to push the wheelbarrow full of manure outside.

"Wait, Jake, let me do that!" Ricki tore herself away from her horse and went over to help the old man. "Can I do anything else for you?" she asked, but Jake just shook his head.

"Thanks for the offer, but today you're just half an hour too late. I'm already finished."

"Oh, I'm really sorry. I overslept." Ricki said dejectedly.

"That's okay. After all, you don't have to go to school today, so you could sleep in for once." Jake shuffled over to the tack room, put away his pitchfork, and reached for the broom.

"Exactly!" beamed Ricki. "I wish there were more teacher training days! Hey, do you happen to know when the others plan to come by today?"

Jake thought a moment. "I think about two o'clock." Then he laughed. "You're asking me, an old fool, when you kids wanted to meet? Hey, which one of us is supposed to have the better memory? You or me?"

Ricki pushed Diablo's gate open and led her black horse into the corridor so she could groom him.

"Well, that was just a test to see if you're still able to think clearly," she replied. She went to get her grooming box after tying up her horse.

"Oh, sure, a test. I see! You think I'm already senile, don't you?"

"No, Jake! Really! I know you have a great memory." The girl began to brush Diablo's coat vigorously.

"I hope it stays that way," responded the horseman, and he began to sweep the floor silently while Ricki devoted herself fully to Diablo's care. With a quick glance to the side at Holli, she realized that Lillian was going to need a few hours to get her horse white again. He had obviously spent the night lying down, as he often did, and he had rolled in his own manure.

If Lillian has to wash him at noon, we might as well forget about going riding, thought Ricki, so she decided to work on Holli's manure stains when she finished with Diablo. *Actually, I could just groom all the horses, one after the other. I'm really in the mood to do it. Kevin and Cathy wouldn't mind, I'm sure, if they got here and found their animals shining clean.*

Ricki took quite a while brushing Kevin's roan, Sharazan, and Cathy's adopted horse, Rashid. Finally, even the little pony mare, Salina, had a shiny coat, as though she'd been rubbed with polish, and Lillian's donkey, Chico, was spotless as well.

Satisfied, Ricki led the little animal back to his stall and then plopped herself down onto a hay bale in the corridor. She glanced at the big clock on the wall that hung over the tack room.

"That's unbelievable!" She was completely surprised. "It's only nine thirty. Wow, I was really fast! What can I do now?"

Mindlessly, she looked down at her clothes. "Boy do I look like a slob. I guess a shower wouldn't be a bad idea." She got up quickly and put away her grooming kit before she ran back to the house, where she nearly bumped into her mother.

"You smell awful!" said Brigitte Sulai, and wrinkled her nose. She glanced at her filthy daughter.

But Ricki just grinned. "Good morning to you too, Mom!" she answered cheerily as she disappeared in the direction of the bathroom.

"Do you want to go into town with me?" Brigitte called after her.

"Oh, yeah! I'll be ready in twenty minutes," she responded. She was delighted to go shopping with her mother. She might be able to talk her into buying her one of those cool zip-up hoodie sweatshirts with the bright yellow logo on it, and it would make the time go more quickly until her friends got there.

*

Standing under the shower, Ricki remembered that she had forgotten to close the safety clasp on Rashid's gate. Jake had made a point of it with the kids because otherwise the horse could get out easily and start eating the hay out of the bin, which would be way too much oats for the dun-colored horse.

"That's very dangerous!" Jake had warned them. "That's just asking for a colic to happen."

Ricki didn't dare think about what Jake would say to her if he came across Rashid running loose in the stable corridor. She dried herself off quickly, pulled on her jeans, and then rushed out of the bathroom with dripping wet hair. She had to close that bolt before Jake noticed it was open.

When she stepped outside, she was met by a cold wind, which had suddenly developed and chased away the sun.

Well, it is winter, the girl thought and pulled her shoulders up high, shivering.

"Hey, are you crazy?" Brigitte stared in disbelief at her daughter's wet hair, as she was coming back inside. "You can't go outside with soaking wet hair in this weather! Are you trying to get pneumonia?"

Ricki rolled her eyes. *Mothers!*

"I'm going to dry my hair right now. I just had to ..."

"That's enough to make you get sick," scolded Brigitte, who worried constantly about her daughter.

"Yeah, yeah, I know! You can stop now!" Quickly the girl took off her jacket and boots and hurried off to escape Brigitte's sermon.

A short time later, the two of them were on their way into town and Ricki was glad that her mother didn't mention the topic of wet hair again.

*

"Oh terrific! You scrubbed Holli! Thanks a lot, Ricki. That's what I call real friendship!" Lillian grinned at Diablo's owner and smoothed his coat once more with the soft currycomb before she saddled her white horse.

"Where are we going to go?" Cathy wanted to know as she led Rashid out into the stable corridor. Rashid and Salina belonged to Carlotta Mancini, the retired circus rider who operated Mercy Ranch, a home for old and neglected horses.

"We could ride over to Josh's again," suggested Kevin, but Lillian just rolled her eyes.

"Anything but that!"

"Why not?"

"I already got a call this morning that wasn't so hot. Josh thinks I'm jealous because I said that I was getting tired of hearing how great Rebecca is!"

"So, relationship stress times ten, huh?"

"You could say that."

"I think I'm going to have to have a little talk with Josh, just us guys," said Kevin, but the suggestion made Lillian explode.

"I don't need anyone to defend me!" she replied angrily. "If he thinks he needs a new girlfriend, then that's what he should do! But he'd better not think that I'll welcome him back with open arms when he finds out that Rebecca isn't so great."

Cathy grinned. "Maybe she'll find out, too, that Josh isn't so great!" she said and winked.

"I can tell her that! She doesn't need to find out herself!" replied Lillian, nastily.

"Oh, come on, he isn't that bad." Kevin tightened his saddle girth a bit. "After all, it was just a little while ago that you called him the perfect boyfriend!"

"People make mistakes," the sixteen-year-old answered, but she wasn't really convinced of what she said. Deep inside, she still liked Josh as much as ever. It just hurt so much to watch him distance himself more and more from her, and it really did seem as though he was more interested in Rebecca than he was in her.

*

Finally, after putting on their jackets, scarves, and gloves, the friends mounted their horses.

"This wind is icy!" declared Cathy, as they made their way down the snow-shoveled path from the stable. "Maybe we should ride through the woods. At least the trees would give us some shelter from the wind."

Ricki nodded in agreement. "Yeah, I think so too. Let's ride for an hour through the woods. We won't last much longer than that anyway. It's too cold."

*

The horses' hooves sank deep into the snow-covered earth. Even though their steps were softened by the snow, and the other riders thought it was like riding through cotton, Ricki's head was pounding and she had the feeling that her brain was about to explode with every step Diablo took.

"How come you're so quiet all of a sudden?" Kevin asked his girlfriend. For a while she had been sitting silently in her saddle, without commenting or taking part in their conversation.

"I feel a little weird," she replied and pressed her hand against her forehead. "I have a killer headache."

"Should we go back?" Lillian stopped Holli and looked anxiously at Ricki.

"Hmm, if you don't mind," she answered softly. "I think I would really feel better if I could lie down at home."

"No problem! But why didn't you say something before we left? We could have stayed home!"

"It didn't hurt then. The headache just started a little while ago."

"Well, then, let's get going." Kevin nodded sympathetically at Ricki. "Do you think you could stand one last gallop? The ground on this path would be perfect for it. When we get out of the woods, it's going to be slippery. We could really save some time if we went at a quicker pace."

"Sure, I'll be fine."

"Okay, then let's go!" After a glance at the others, Kevin shortened the reins and pressed his calves against Sharazan's flanks. The powerful roan galloped away, followed by the other horses.

The pine branches, laden with snow, hung down heavily and even blocked the narrow path in places. The young riders had to duck often and bend down low over their horses' necks to avoid being swept out of their saddles.

Normally Ricki would have loved this ride on her wonderful horse, but today every step was torture. She longed to be home in her bed instead of bucking an icy wind.

Muffled by the snow, Diablo's hooves beat on the ground. Rocking gently to the pace of Diablo's gait, Ricki was tempted to close her eyes and give in to her fatigue. Suddenly, she jumped, startled by Cathy's screaming behind her. Her head snapped around and she realized that her girlfriend was sitting crookedly in the saddle and trying to regain her balance. Rashid had probably slid and was just able to regain his footing before going down.

When Ricki turned her head forward again, a thick branch whipped across her face.

"Aaargh!" she screamed in pain and pulled furiously on Diablo's reins. The black horse came to a full stop almost immediately.

"Whoa, Holli!" Lillian tried to stop her horse, so that he wouldn't bump into Diablo. Cathy managed to stop Rashid in time as well, and Kevin turned Sharazan and trotted back to them.

"What happened to you guys?" he asked, out of breath. However, when he looked at his girlfriend and saw her face, he couldn't say anything at first. Then he asked, "Didn't you see that big branch? You look like someone who's just been hit with a whip across your forehead!"

Ricki pressed her hands against her face as she tried to relieve the pain. But she couldn't prevent the tears from pouring down her cheeks.

"What an idiot I am," she said through clenched teeth. "I just didn't see it. Oh, man, it really hurts!"

Upset and worried, Cathy, Lillian, and Kevin stared at their friend, who was trying to open her eyes, despite the fact that her eyelids had begun to swell. All she could manage was a tiny crack.

16

"I can't open my eyes. It hurts too much!"

"Then just keep them closed and spare them," Kevin said. He positioned Sharazan beside the black horse. "Hold on to his mane. I'm going to lead Diablo." He reached for the horse's reins and pulled them over his head.

"Are you ready? Can we get started?" he asked again just to be sure, and when Ricki nodded, resigned, he let Sharazan walk forward slowly. Carefully, he led the two horses around anything uneven in their path and he was glad when they finally left the woods. He knew that it would only be another fifteen minutes until they were back in the Sulais' stable.

"I think I can ride by myself now," Ricki said after about five minutes. The pain around her eyes had let up a little and she was able to open them enough so she could see where she was going.

"Are you sure? I mean, you still can't see, and it's no trouble for me to lead Diablo."

Ricki shook her head. "It'll be okay. Diablo knows the way and he can follow you," she said, determined. She didn't say anything about being dizzy and sick to her stomach.

"Well, okay." Kevin pulled the reins back over Diablo's head and handed them back to Ricki.

Ricki shrugged her shoulders and shivered. The icy wind was becoming stronger and stronger, but her head felt as though it was on fire.

*

When the friends finally reached the Sulai farm, Ricki slid weakly out of the saddle. At first she had to lean on Diablo to keep from falling over. Her legs felt like rubber and she was glad when Kevin came over to her and put his arms around her for support.

"Cathy and Lillian will take our horses into the stable and I'm going to take you into the house first. You have to lie down right away," he said in a voice clearly not willing to accept any arguments.

Ricki nodded in agreement and let Kevin lead her.

Brigitte Sulai turned pale when she saw her daughter.

Ricki was sitting on the bench in the mudroom, miserable, as Kevin was pulling off her boots.

"For heaven's sakes, Ricki! What happened to your face? Honey, you look awful!" Carefully, Brigitte stroked her daughter's hair away from her face and stared at the red welts.

"I ran into a branch. It just suddenly appeared and I couldn't get out of the way."

"I hate this riding business!" scolded Brigitte, shaking her head. "I keep telling you, it is, and always will be, a dangerous sport! Why can't you do something else?"

"Please, Mom," Ricki groaned. At the moment, she didn't feel like talking about riding with her mother. "You can get hit in the face with a ball playing tennis, and anyway, that branch didn't have anything to do with riding!"

For the first time, Brigitte realized that her daughter wasn't looking at her while she spoke.

"Open your eyes," she ordered. However, Ricki just shook her head slowly.

"I can't. It's as if an invisible hand is pressing down on the lids," she tried to explain. "And I have such a bad headache. I'd like to lie down, Mom." She got up a little shakily and Kevin immediately went to her to support her.

Brigitte took a deep breath. "Okay. Kevin, take her upstairs. I'll be right there."

"Sure, Mrs. Sulai." Carefully, the boy led his girlfriend up to her room, where she let herself fall onto the bed immediately.

"Don't you want your mom to help you get undressed first?" asked Kevin, glancing at the soaking-wet riding pants. Ricki just mumbled something that sounded like, "I can't anymore!" So Kevin sat down on the the chair next to her bed, and took her hand and stroked it awkwardly. Hardly two minutes later, Ricki's mother came through the door.

Worried, she looked at her daughter and sent Kevin outside. Then she began to take off Ricki's snow-wet clothing.

"Why do you do these things?" she said softly, when the girl was finally dressed in her warm pajamas and, exhausted, had fallen into a deep sleep. Tenderly, Brigitte stroked her wounded face and suddenly realized how hot it was.

"You have a fever! Didn't I tell you that you shouldn't ride in winter without a hat? And then this morning you went outside with soaking wet hair! This is just what I was afraid of. I knew you'd be sorry!" With an anxious sigh, Brigitte got up and tiptoed out of the room. She went downstairs to the kitchen to make her daughter a pot of tea.

Kevin went back to the stable, downhearted. Lillian and Cathy had already unsaddled the horses and were just cleaning out their hooves.

"And? Is she lying down? Does she feel better?" Cathy asked.

"She's lying down, but I don't think she looks good," replied Kevin unhappily. "Her mother gave her a good talking to, about how dangerous riding is, and everything."

"Well, that's fabulous! The same old stuff, huh? Why can't Mrs. Sulai understand that every sport can be dangerous?" Lillian shook her head angrily. She was so glad that her parents weren't like that.

"I think that's because she's frightened of horses herself," suggested Cathy. Her girlfriend just waved that theory aside.

"Oh, come on. Diablo can't be blamed for that dumb branch!"

Kevin snorted loudly. "That's what Ricki said too, but the way I see it, Mrs. Sulai has a completely different viewpoint."

"That's obvious!" Lillian led Holli into his stall and then turned to do Diablo's hooves. "It's always your fault, you poor thing, no matter what happens to Ricki," she said to him and stroked his forehead lovingly. "Maybe someday Mrs. Sulai will see what a wonderful creature you really are!"

Kevin shut his eyes tightly. "I don't think it's Diablo that's the problem for Ricki's mother. It's horses in general that scare her. Why do you think she makes such a drama out of it every time Harry wants to ride Salina? After all, the little pony is absolutely safe. She would never get out of line, not to mention kick or bite or bolt. Even so, Harry always has to jump through a hundred hoops before she finally allows him, against her better judgment, to get up on Salina's back, even for ten minutes and with someone supervising him."

"That's true." Cathy, whose mother was also easily frightened, whistled through her teeth. "I don't think Mrs. Sulai will ever be able to get over this fear. Poor Ricki. I don't want to be around to hear all the sermons she'll have to listen to as soon as she wakes up."

"Me neither," replied Kevin. Silently he devoted himself to his roan, who was bored and impatiently scratching in the dirt with his hoof. Sharazan glanced enviously at Holli, who was already standing at his hayrack, chewing contentedly.

Chapter 2

Lillian was trying to maneuver her bike over the snowy
road. She'd given a lot of thought as to whether or not
she should go to the Western ranch, especially since Josh
accused her of being angry with him lately. But then she
remembered all the wonderful moments they'd shared
together. They'd been so happy riding side by side through
the woods. And at the county fair they'd been in complete
harmony and there were no signs that anything would ever
change their relationship. But ever since Rebecca showed
up at the ranch, Josh had seemed like a different person.

Rebecca!

Lillian took a deep breath, and suddenly she knew
why she had wanted to go to the ranch today so urgently.
It wasn't Josh she wanted to see there, it was Rebecca.
Lillian wanted to know what the girl who had stolen
her boyfriend looked like. She couldn't imagine that
it was only Rebecca's riding skills that Josh found so
fascinating. She was convinced that there was a lot more

behind this. She was probably pretty, and all of the guys at the ranch probably liked her. She was probably the perfect Western rider too, which is something Lillian would never be. How could Josh be such a jerk and get drawn in by her? How could he risk losing their wonderful relationship so easily?

Lillian pressed her lips together tightly. What was she doing? After all, she didn't even know Rebecca, and here she was making judgments about her. But the fear of losing Josh wouldn't allow her to give the girl the benefit of the doubt.

"I hate you!" Lillian snarled, and pedaled furiously. "You're trying to take Josh away from me!" She wiped her eyes hastily. She didn't want to cry, but she couldn't prevent a few tears from rolling down her cheeks.

When she finally saw the ranch in the distance, Lillian stopped her bike and stared at the wide expanse of paddocks surrounding the stable.

A herd of pinto horses stood there peacefully, looking for a few blades of grass under the snow and grazing slowly. What an idyllic picture!

However, Lillian's heart beat more wildly when she discovered that Josh's Cherish was among the horses. So Josh wasn't out riding.

I wonder if he's in the stable? Lillian asked herself. Or maybe his father needed him in his riding shop and he would have to find the time later to exercise his horse.

For a moment, she considered going back home. But then Rebecca's name flashed in her mind's eye and, determined, she kept going. She was going to try to talk with Rebecca. If she got the impression that something was going on between her and Josh, then ... Yeah, what then? Would she tell her off? Would she lose her temper? Would she start a fight, or would she say nothing and simply walk away?

A thousand thoughts went through Lillian's head as she parked her bike in the rack in front of the ranch. She had no idea what she was going to do if she ran into Rebecca.

She stood there undecided and suddenly she wasn't so sure that she should go into the stable. Did she have to do this to herself?

Yes! You have to! she heard her inner voice telling her. *You need to be sure about what your relationship to Josh is going to be like in the future!*

"Yeah, yeah, I know," murmured Lillian and, gathering all her courage, she walked hesitantly toward the large wooden swinging door that would take her inside the stable.

She could hear happy laughter coming from inside. She took one more deep breath before she entered the building.

*

After Kevin had looked in on Ricki once more and saw that she was sleeping soundly, he and Cathy decided to bike over to Mercy Ranch to visit Carlotta.

"What made us think of coming out to the ranch in this miserable weather?" grumbled Cathy. Now, in retrospect, she imagined how much cozier and warmer it would have been in her room at home, and could have kicked herself for leaving it.

"What else could we do on such a lousy day?" asked Kevin, who couldn't stop thinking about Ricki. "She didn't look good."

"Who?"

"Who do you think? Ricki, of course!"

"Hmmm," responded Cathy, as she avoided an icy stone on the path. "I think she didn't feel well even before we started."

"I hope she doesn't get sick," replied Kevin with an anxious look.

"Oh, Ricki is tough. I bet she'll be fine by tomorrow," answered Cathy and was relieved when Mercy Ranch appeared before them.

"I wonder if Hal's there today?" she thought out loud. Kevin glanced at her in surprise.

"Hal? Don't tell me you have a crush on him?"

Cathy turned red. "That's ridiculous! What are you talking about?" she asked, obviously embarrassed, and she avoided looking at Kevin, who was grinning broadly.

"Just as I thought. You always looked moonstruck at him during that week we spent with the guests at the ranch."

"That's not true!"

"Of course it's true. Everybody noticed it," teased Kevin.

"No, really? You guys all noticed that?"

"Of course!"

"Oh, no, how embarrassing!"

Kevin laughed. "I think everybody knew it except Hal!"

Cathy sighed. "How come the people who are involved with it are the last to notice?"

"Probably because they're thinking with their hearts, and not their heads."

"Thanks a lot!" Cathy gave Kevin a look of playful

despair, but then she started to laugh too. "Now I know why you're always so weird!"

"Exactly! Weird but happy."

"How long have you and Ricki been together?"

Kevin puffed out his cheeks. "I have no idea. I'd have to think about it. Anyway, a long time."

"Wow, you boys are so bad! I'll bet Ricki could give me the exact date."

"Oh, sure! You girls are just different from us. You can remember the most unimportant things in the world, and we concentrate on the important things in life!"

"Oh, right, are you telling me that it's unimportant for you to know how long you and Ricki have been dating? You can't be serious, can you?"

Kevin shook his head. "You can't look at it that way, Cathy," he said after a short pause for reflection. "Of course the time with Ricki is important to me. Very important, but actually, but it's not about whether we've been together since yesterday, for a month, or for a year. The main thing is that we're happy together. I think the present is always the most important time."

In the meantime, the two of them had arrived at Carlotta's ranch and they parked their bikes.

"Come to think of it, you might just be right," Cathy had to admit. She pulled out a handkerchief and blew her nose heartily.

"You don't have to cry about it," grinned Kevin and put his arm around his friend to comfort her.

Together they ran over to the stable, where Carlotta and her helpers were distributing the evening hay rations.

"Hi, you two! What are you doing here? I didn't think you'd come today," the Mercy Ranch owner greeted them warmly, leaning on a pitchfork.

"Well, we just missed you so much," teased Kevin and winked at Kieran and Bev, who came walking out of the feed-storage room. "Hi! Everything okay with you guys?"

"Of course!" Kieran laughed. "How about you two? Everything all right?"

"Well, not exactly." Kevin's face clouded over.

"How come? What happened?" Bev looked questioningly at the two visitors.

"Ricki's in bed, recovering from a riding accident; Lillian's having problems in her relationship with Josh; and Mrs. Sulai had another one of her fits about horses. All together, I'd say this day has been somewhat chaotic."

Carlotta frowned. "What about Ricki? What happened? Is she hurt?"

"We went riding earlier and Ricki got hit in the face with a branch. And that's the way her face looks. When she got home, she had a fever. I think she just caught a cold. Nothing serious, I bet, but Mrs. Sulai has made Diablo responsible yet again."

Carlotta sighed. "I'll visit Brigitte in the next few days and put in a good word for the black horse. Tell her I said hello, and wish Ricki a speedy recovery from me. I'm sure she'll be back in shape soon."

"I really hope so." Kevin's glance fell on Cathy, who was snuggling with Hadrian, one of the horses Carlotta had saved from being put down.

"Is Hal here today?" the boy asked innocently, and bit his lip when he saw how quickly Cathy turned toward him. Her eyes spoke volumes.

"Hal? No idea where he is today. Actually, he should have been here half an hour ago. Maybe he got stuck in the snow," replied Bev. "Why do you ask?"

"No reason. It's just unusual for him not to be here."

"You're so lucky!" Cathy whispered to Kevin. "I'd have strangled you if you'd said anything!"

Kevin winked at her like an accomplice. "Don't worry. I would never do anything like that!"

"Oh, right! I know you!"

"Exactly!"

"As long as you're here, you could help us muck out the stalls." Bev came with two pitchforks and pushed one into the hands of each of the visitors.

"Of course we'll help," responded Kevin, and started walking toward the first stall.

"Working is fun. I could watch you two for hours," grinned Kieran.

"Oh no, you don't! Get going. You can relax at home," said Bev as she pushed the boy toward the heavy hay bales. "You're always saying that you're so strong, aren't you? Then show us your muscles and carry these over for me, please."

"Certainly, Madame! At your service." Kieran made a little bow and then got started with the work.

Carlotta grinned. She was really pleased that the young people helped her every day in the stable, and also that they all got along so well, without anyone complaining.

"You all have the right attitude with animals, and I think that's wonderful," the retired circus performer, who had devoted her life to old and ailing horses, always told the kids. At the end of the day, there weren't many things the kids would rather do than spend their free time with Carlotta in the stable.

*

Ricki was still sleeping soundly. She had pulled the blanket up to her chin, and even in her dreams she had the feeling that she was freezing, although her body was hot.

She kept seeing her mother in front of her, shaking her finger at her accusingly.

"Didn't I tell you that you'd get sick if you went outside with wet hair? That's what you get!"

Ricki groaned in her sleep and pressed her hands over her ears.

Suddenly, she was sitting on Diablo and there was a beautiful snowy avenue opening up in front of her.

I've never been here before, she thought happily. She discovered that only the trees were covered with snow, but the rest of the landscape was green.

"Let's go for a gallop, boy," called Ricki gaily and she pressed her thighs against her horse's belly, but Diablo stepped backward, and she was unable to get him to take even one step forward.

"Hey, what are you doing? Don't tell me you're afraid of snow?" the girl laughed at her horse. "Come on, let's go!"

Kevin rushed past her on Sharazan, right toward the broad street, followed by Cathy on Rashid, and Lillian on Doc Holliday.

"What are you waiting for, Ricki? This is the best stretch for galloping that we've ever had," Holli's rider called over her shoulder.

"I know," grumbled the girl, and she started to get angry because Diablo was misbehaving so much.

Kevin had already reached the end of the broad street and was waving wildly.

"I think that's really mean," Ricki scolded her horse. "You're ruining the most wonderful gallop of our lives!"

Diablo put his ears flat against his head, then he thundered ahead like a racehorse out of the starting gate.

"All right!" Ricki was delighted and bent down low over her horse's neck. Tree after tree flew by, but suddenly she noticed that the street was becoming narrower and narrower until it was hardly as wide as a footpath.

Ricki tried in vain to stop Diablo, but the animal just raced ahead toward his stable mates. Low-hanging branches beat against Ricki's face and back, and soon she was screaming in pain.

"It's Diablo's fault!" Once again she heard the accusing voice of her mother. "Riding is dangerous! You should choose another activity! Diablo will only make you unhappy! He's to blame!"

Ricki shook her head wildly. "NO!" she wanted to scream, but she couldn't say anything.

Again and again, the branches beat against her body, and there wasn't an inch of it that wasn't in pain. Horrified, Ricki saw that the trees in front of her were forming into a wall, but before Diablo could bang into the green wall, the girl sat bolt upright in bed, panting, covered in sweat, and terrified by the images in her nightmare. She wanted to open her eyes, get back to reality, but the lids were still so swollen that Ricki couldn't even see any light.

Slowly, the girl let herself sink back down onto her pillow. Every single bone was aching.

What a horrible dream, she thought, upset, and then she was shocked to actually hear her mother's voice.

"Ricki, you're awake! Do you feel any better?" Brigitte Sulai sat down on the edge of the bed and tenderly placed her hand on Ricki's forehead.

"You still have a fever," she said, frowning. "Drink a little tea first, and then I'll go downstairs and see what kind of medicine I have on hand."

Carefully, she supported Ricki's head while she held the cup of tea to her mouth.

"Drink," she ordered. "There's a lot of vitamin C in that and you need it to get better!"

Ricki made a face after only the first sip. "EEEEEW, this isn't tea! This is pure hot lemon juice! Yuck! This is making me sick!"

"Stop complaining."

"You don't have to drink it!"

"I don't walk around outside in the middle of winter with soaking wet hair!"

Ricki jumped, because her mother's voice sounded just like the voice in her dream. Slowly, dream and reality melted together into a thick layer of cotton that surrounded Ricki, and a few moments later she was asleep again.

"Hello, Lillian. We haven't seen you around here for a long time!" Alex and Marty waved to the girl as she entered the stable of the Western ranch.

"Hey, you two." Lillian tried to sound as casual as possible. "I thought I'd come by and see if there's anything new happening around here."

Alex grinned. "New? Doesn't Joe keep you up-to-date?"

Joe ...? Lillian still hadn't gotten used to the fact that Josh's buddies called him Joe.

"Nope, not really, but we don't see each other that often right now," she admitted hesitantly. "Somehow we both seem to have a chronic lack of time."

Marty looked at her in astonishment. "Well, Joe has plenty of time. He hangs out here every day for hours! So it can't be his fault."

Lillian jumped at the thought. *So that's how it is,* she thought. *He's at the ranch for hours, and he told me that he has to help his father in the evenings! That's just great!*

"Do you guys know if he's coming here today?" she asked.

"No idea," replied Alex, "but I think so. It would be the first time he didn't show up." He glanced at his watch. "My guess is he'll be here in about half an hour. Would you like a soda?"

"Hmmm, yes, thanks."

"Well, then, come along, little lady. We'll go sit in the snack bar for a while. Marty, are you coming with us?" Alex put his hand on his friend's shoulder, but he shook his head.

"No. You know there's something else I want to do," he grinned suggestively and Alex understood.

"Okay, then, see you later!" He winked at him, and then he gave Lillian a sign to follow him to the clubhouse and into the snack bar.

"What does Marty have to do that's so important?" Lillian asked as soon as she was seated with Alex at one of the rustic wooden tables. She sipped at her soda.

Alex laughed and waved her question aside. "Oh, you know Marty, Mr. Cool. When we get new talent here at the ranch, he always has to try his luck!"

Lillian made a face. "New talent? What's that?"

"Hey, can't you take a joke at all today? What's wrong? I can tell that something's not right with you. You're so different today. Does it have anything to do with Joe? Is he giving you trouble?"

Lillian turned her head to the side and didn't know what to say.

"Well, say something, girl! You know, future vets always have time for a quick free diagnosis," he joked.

"Yeah, I've heard that."

Alex looked at her completely baffled. "Oh no, are people talking about me already? I'd better be careful, so I don't get a bad reputation." He grinned mischievously, and Lillian couldn't help smiling at him. Alex was an extremely nice guy, and Lillian could remember when Ricki had gotten a crush on him. Kevin had been furious, and they'd almost broken up over it.

"Tell me about Marty." Lillian tried to change the subject.

"Good grief, Marty is so unimportant if you're having problems." Alex rolled his eyes. "He's been asking out our newest member, but she has absolutely no interest in him."

"Is the girl's name Rebecca?" asked Lillian, just a little too quickly, so that Alex became suspicious.

"Oh, so that's what this is about. Yeah, her name is Rebecca, and apparently you know all about her."

"I don't know anything about her, but Josh talks about her so often that I'm beginning to worry, that ..."

"That what? That he likes her?" Alex said exactly what Lillian was trying to say and it made her turn bright red.

"That's what I thought. You wouldn't have come here to the ranch for no reason! After all, we all know that you don't like Western-style riding!"

"Who says so?" Lillian turned and her eyes were blazing. "Joe!"

"Josh said that about me? Why is he doing that? I never said that!"

"You didn't?" Alex asked, interested.

"No! Never! It's just that I have a horse that I can't ride Western style, and that's why I prefer riding English. But I never said that I don't like Western. That's crazy! Josh knows how much it fascinates me, but he's mad because I don't go to all his shows." Lillian took a deep breath. She felt hurt and betrayed by Josh. Why was her boyfriend saying things about her that weren't true? She couldn't believe it. What had happened to him? He used to be completely different.

"Hmmm." Alex looked pensively at her, but then he just shrugged his shoulders. "I'd prefer it if the two of you would talk this out between yourselves. You know, Lillian, I like you a lot, but Joe has been my friend for a long, long time, and I don't want to interfere. If I had thought about it a little longer, it would probably have been better not to say anything. Now it looks like I've made it worse for you two. I'm really sorry."

Lillian looked at him with tears in her eyes. "No, no! Don't worry, Alex, that's okay. At least now I know where I stand with him."

"Hey, maybe he was just having a bad day when he said that."

"Alex, I told you, it's okay! I've felt for a long time that things between us aren't like they used to be, and I've asked myself why. Tell me, does he have a crush on Rebecca? That's all I want to know right now, and to be honest, that's why I came here today."

"What a question!" Alex was beginning to feel very uncomfortable. Just a few days ago, Josh had told him that he found Rebecca more than just nice. And when Alex then asked him about Lillian, Josh had just waved his concerns aside.

"So, tell me. What's going on?" Lillian wasn't going to let it rest. If anyone could give her an answer, besides Josh, Alex could. But all of a sudden he didn't feel like talking. He could feel Lillian's pain, her disappointment, and he just couldn't bear to hurt her feelings even more.

He was almost glad when the snack bar door opened, and Jackie and Crystal rushed in.

"Alex, you have to come over to the stalls! Rebecca is having problems with her mare."

"What kind of problems?"

"Apparently Shakira lost her footing and now she's limping on her front left leg. Rebecca would like you to examine her mare."

"Tell her I'll be right there," replied Alex, with a long look at Lillian. He waited until the two others had left the room.

"Are you coming?"

At first Lillian wanted to say no, but her curiosity about Rebecca won out. She nodded and got up.

But only when they had reached the stable did she realize that he still hadn't answered her question.

Sometimes no answer is the same as an answer, she thought sadly. But then she straightened her shoulders and steeled herself for the meeting with her supposed rival.

*

"Oh, Alex, it's really nice of you to take a look at Shakira," Rebecca said. "She lost her footing and I just hope that she didn't do herself any real damage. You know that we wanted to participate in the reining show this coming weekend."

Alex nodded. "Yeah, you told me that yesterday. Lead your darling out into the hallway. Oh, by the way, this is Lillian ... Joe's girlfriend."

"Oh, hello Lillian!" Rebecca smiled at her briefly. "Excuse me, but I have to take care of my horse."

"No problem." Lillian was mad at herself that her voice sounded so hoarse all of a sudden.

She took a good look at Rebecca and tried to read her face. Especially when Rebecca looked at her. But even though she tried her best, she couldn't see anything that would have confirmed her fears about Josh.

Rebecca made a very friendly, open, and, as Lillian had to admit, pleasant impression. She didn't seem to have any hang-ups toward Lillian, and it didn't seem likely that she was planning to steal Josh from her. So what was it that had caused Josh to become so distant?

Is it possible that it's all my fault? Lillian dared to think, but then shook her head.

No!

If he's begun to say negative things about me, then he must be looking for reasons to explain to his friends why he no longer likes me.

I'll find out! Lillian swore to herself before she hastily said good-bye. She couldn't stand to be at the ranch any longer. As she was running outside she almost bumped into Josh, who was just coming in through the same door.

They stood across from one another and looked at each other in embarrassment. Neither one of them had imagined that they would run into the other just then.

"Hi," said Lillian, a little shyly. She remembered that in other times they would have given each other a big hug, overjoyed.

"Hello, sweetheart, what are you doing here?" Josh's voice sounded a little surprised, which hurt the girl's feelings.

"I ... I thought you'd be glad to see me if I came to visit. After all, we haven't seen each other in over a week."

"Hmmm, yeah, it's nice to see you!" Josh glanced a little impatiently at his watch. "But I promised Rebecca that we would train together for the show this weekend. She's probably already waiting for me. I'm sorry, Lillian, but I don't have any time for you right now. I didn't know you were coming."

Lillian could feel the tears building up, but the last thing she wanted was to show Josh how she really felt.

"You're going to have to train alone. Rebecca's mare is lame. Alex is examining her right now as we speak."

Josh frowned. "Shakira is lame? That can't be true! We've trained so hard and we would have had a good chance at winning on Saturday. If Becky can't participate, our team's victory will be in trouble. Hey, I'm sorry, but I really have to go and see what's what. I'll see you sometime, okay?" He gave Lillian a quick peck on the cheek and was gone before she had a chance to say good-bye.

Josh had hardly disappeared behind the stable door when Lillian ran to her bike and rode off as though a wasp had stung her. Tears rolled down her cheeks. She knew she had lost Josh.

Chapter 3

Cathy was overjoyed when Hal turned up at Mercy Ranch.

"Well, what luck!" quipped Kevin, who had not missed the fact that his riding companion was beaming.

"Be quiet!" Cathy warned him.

"I'll be as silent as the grave," he grinned. However, Cathy couldn't get over the feeling that Kevin was just waiting for an opportunity to say something that was sure to embarrass her.

"Swear that you won't say anything!"

"Hey, I never swear!"

"I'm going to strangle you."

"Hey, you guys. I haven't seen you two in ages!" Hal approached them happily and clapped Kevin on the shoulder. He didn't seem to notice that Cathy, her face bright red, was giving Kevin pleading looks.

"Today was total chaos at our house. My mother was going to drive me here, but the car wouldn't start. And my father was waiting at his office for my mother to come and pick him up and drive him to the doctor. Of course, that didn't happen either. My little sister, who was supposed to be driven to her flute lesson, had a fit because today was the last rehearsal before her school recital. So I had to take my sister to her lesson, while my mother tried to find a garage that would repair the car as quickly as possible. Dad was furious that he missed his appointment. To be honest, I'm glad I'm here and out of that stress at home. I'm sorry that I couldn't get here earlier and help you."

Kevin grinned. "There must be something in the air that's making everything crazy today," he said. Then he walked away to get the stable broom.

Cathy watched him go. How could he leave her alone with Hal?

"How long have you guys been here?" Hal asked pleasantly. However, Cathy was still watching Kevin, who had disappeared into the tack room.

"Cathy?"

The girl whipped her head around. "Yes?"

"I asked you how long you've been here."

"Umm, about an hour and a half, I guess." Cathy's voice sounded like a creaking door hinge. Up to now, she had never had a problem talking to Hal, but today she was afraid she couldn't say a word without having a panic attack. She felt that he would sense what was going through her mind.

"You're acting so weird today," Hal declared. "Is something wrong?"

Uh-oh! Cathy swallowed hard and stared past him in embarrassment. "What do you mean?" she asked hoarsely.

"That's what I'm asking you," laughed Hal. "I thought maybe you could tell me!"

"What do you mean by 'weird?'"

"Just different, somehow, than the way you usually are."

"Hmmm," Cathy responded. She had a thousand thoughts going through her head, but she was incapable of producing one normal sentence.

"You seem to be in a funny mood today," Hal announced after a brief silence. Then he turned to his favorite four-legged friend, Jonah. "Whatever! Everybody has a bad day sometime!"

Cathy balled her hands into fists behind her back.

Bad day! she thought. *If you only knew how good the day is, now that you're here! Oh, I am such an idiot!*

"Who wants tea and fresh apple cake?" Carlotta's voice floated through the stable door. There was enthusiastic approval everywhere. "Then come with me. I think we could all do with a little warming up."

Cathy stood still for another minute, lost in thought, and watched Hal join the others. As though he sensed her eyes on his back, he turned abruptly and looked right at her.

"What's up? Aren't you coming?" he asked.

"Yeah, yeah, I just wanted to ... well, I thought ..." the girl stammered, searching for an explanation.

Hal looked at her closely, and then he walked back to her.

Cathy's heart was beating so wildly she was afraid the boy would hear it.

"You're really being strange today. Come on, tell me

what's wrong. Maybe I can help you." His eyes, filled with worry, made Cathy's knees weak.

Yesssss, she cried to herself.

"No, no," she said instead, and avoided looking at Hal.

Why don't you just tell him you're crazy about him? she heard her inner voice say.

Hal's eyes stayed on Cathy, and suddenly he felt as if he were looking at her for the first time. Funny that he had never noticed before how pretty she was.

"Want to go for a walk?" he asked all of a sudden.

Cathy had the feeling that she was going to faint with happiness. "Don't you want any tea and cake?" she asked hoarsely.

Hal laughed softly. "Do you?"

The girl shook her head silently. No way would she have been able to eat even a bite right then.

"Then let's take that walk." Hal pulled up the zipper on his thick parka as he watched Cathy pull on her gloves with trembling hands. It was then that he realized what was going on with her, and a wave of happiness overwhelmed him.

"Are you ready?" he asked softly. When Cathy answered him with a quick nod, he looked into her eyes deeply, reached for her hand, pressed it lightly, and kept holding it as they walked slowly down the stable corridor and outside.

Cathy felt as though she were in a trance. Feelings were whirling inside her that she'd never felt for a boy before.

This is just too good to be true, she thought, imagining that Hal liked her just as much as she liked him.

"What's keeping Cathy and Hal? Didn't they hear me?" Carlotta asked, in the warm kitchen of Mercy Ranch.

Kevin just grinned to himself. Just a moment ago, he had happened to glance out the window and had seen the two of them walking hand in hand toward the paddock.

"I don't think we need to wait for those two," he replied, winking and pointing outside. "They are, um, occupied at the moment!"

Carlotta squinted and tried to see out of the foggy window. Then she smiled.

"Well, of all things! Who would have thought it!"

Bev and Kieran looked at each other perplexed, but then they too understood.

"One more couple, if you can believe that!" sighed Bev and made a face. "Romeo, oh Romeo," she quipped, and Kieran just shook his head.

"Darling Juliet, if you think that I am going to drink a poisoned potion for you, you're mistaken! But why don't you take a sip of this delicious beverage, called herbal tea, to bring you back to your senses!"

"Idiot! You're so unromantic!" Bev turned to Carlotta. "Men are the worst!"

*

Lillian had ridden back to the Sulai farm. She wouldn't have been able to stand her mother's questions.

Sniffing, she now stood in Holli's stall brushing his coat.

Jake, who had been watching her for a while, approached her and leaned his arms over the half door of the stall.

"You're going to rub a hole in his coat if you don't start moving your brush to another spot, Lillian."

Startled, she jumped. She stared first at the old stable hand, and then back at the place on Holli's coat that she had been working on for at least half an hour, her mind on other things.

"What's wrong? Where are the others? I'm not used to so much quiet in here and just one of you in the stalls."

Lillian forced herself to put on an innocent face, but she didn't quite manage it.

"Everything's fine, Jake. Really! Cathy and Kevin rode over to Carlotta's. I'm sure they'll be back soon, and Ricki's probably still asleep."

Jake frowned. "Ricki's sleeping? In the middle of the day? What do you young folks do at night that makes you so sleepy during the day?" He grinned, but Lillian looked at him seriously.

"I think Ricki has a bad case of the flu, and the branch that hit her in the face while we were out riding finished her off. Her whole face was swollen when we got back. Didn't you hear anything about it?"

Jake's laughter died on his lips as soon as Lillian told him about Ricki.

"No! How come nobody told me? So Ricki had another stroke of bad luck riding. Oh no! Just what her mother needs to keep her worrying."

"Yeah, unfortunately." Lillian turned back to her horse.

"Then I'm going to go over there right now and see how the patient's doing. Thanks for filling me in. No one ever

44

tells me anything!" he grumbled and walked out of the stable in a bad mood. In a few minutes he was in the Sulais' kitchen, confronting Ricki's mother.

"What's up with Ricki? How is she?" Jake asked Mrs. Sulai. "It isn't anything serious, is it?"

"She's still sleeping, Jake. I was just in her room. She still has a fever and her face looks pretty bruised," replied Brigitte seriously. "Someday, riding is going to ruin her! She keeps having accidents, and I am worried sick. I'm never calm when she's out riding Diablo." She looked at Jake accusingly. "Why did you have to give her that wretched horse?"

Jake bit his lips. How many times had he listened to her accusing him of that?

"You're forgetting, Brigitte, that only happened after we discussed it with Marcus. And, after all, your husband must have discussed it with you as well. So, don't be unfair!"

"Oh, I know. And how many times do you think that I've regretted that I gave him my permission?"

"You're exaggerating, Brigitte! You know very well that Diablo is a wonderful, intelligent horse. Why do you always blame him when something happens to your daughter? Do you think it was Diablo that made that branch hang down over the path, or that he ran underneath it on purpose? And anyway, something like that can only happen when the rider isn't concentrating! Who knows what Ricki was looking at! One thing's for sure, she wasn't looking ahead, the way she should have been when she's riding." He paused briefly, and Brigitte just looked

45

at him as though she had no idea what the old man was talking about.

"Did you ask her yourself how it happened? I mean ..."

"No, I haven't had the chance to do that yet, but that's not important. If it were Diablo's fault, she would never tell me the truth, she would just invent some other story."

"It was definitely not the horse's fault, Brigitte! Don't be so stubborn!"

"I'm not stubborn! I'm just worried about my daughter. I'm afraid that someday something really serious will happen to her, more serious than just getting hit with a branch. Can't you understand that, Jake?"

The old man said nothing. Of course he could understand that a mother would worry about her children, but she shouldn't be so overprotective. If he hadn't been one hundred percent sure that Diablo was the right horse for Ricki, he wouldn't have given her the wonderful animal. If only Brigitte would finally accept that.

While he silently studied Brigitte, it became clear to him that today any words would be in vain, and so he turned away from her.

"I'll go, then. Please tell Ricki, when she wakes up, that I wish her a speedy recovery."

Brigitte nodded silently and watched the old man leave the house. After a while, she turned and slowly climbed the creaking stairs. Maybe Ricki had wakened and would want to eat a little something.

*

"I'm really crazy about you," Hal was saying to Cathy as he

squeezed her hand. "I don't know why it struck me today, because I've known you for a while, but it just did."

Cathy looked at the boy and tried to regain her composure. No one had ever said anything like that to her before. Actually, if she were honest, no one had ever told her that he liked her, and the feeling was so intense that she would never be able to express it in words.

"I ... I feel the same way about you, too," she replied, squeezing his hand in return.

Smiling, Hal gave her a quick kiss on the forehead and looked at her with an expression she'd never seen on him before.

"We should probably go back to the others," he said. "They probably miss us."

Cathy nodded, even though she wished this moment would never end.

Hand in hand, the two of them slowly walked back to the house, enjoying every second of being together.

*

"Oh, romance is wonderful," teased Kieran, as Cathy and Hal, their faces bright red with embarrassment, entered the kitchen.

"Of course," grinned Hal, letting go of Cathy's hand. "You're just jealous!"

"Yes! No! Well, maybe a little," admitted Kieran with a twinkle in his eye.

"Hmmm, Bev and Lina are still unattached!" remarked Kevin seriously.

"Oh, man, Lina! She's going to have a fit when she finds out that you two are together. She's had a crush on you forever!" Bev exploded, and then clapped her hand over her mouth.

"Really?" Hal laughed. "I didn't realize I was so popular!"

"Nice work!" Kevin gave him the thumbs up. "Where is Lina today?"

"She's grounded for a few days because she cut out on her math test," responded Bev.

"Oh, that's not good! Hey, Cathy, we'd better get going. It'll be dark soon, and we wanted to check on Ricki," said Kevin, glancing at the two lovebirds.

Cathy sighed. *What timing,* she thought. *I'd so much rather stay here with Hal.*

"I have to go, too. My little sister is probably waiting for me to pick her up," responded Hal, making it less difficult for Cathy to separate from her new boyfriend.

"Get home safely," said Carlotta to the three as they left the house.

"Okay," called Kevin over his shoulder. "Cathy, if you don't come soon, I'm leaving without you!" he warned, laughing, as he got on his bike.

"All right, Kevin. You don't need to threaten me. I'm coming!"

"Bye, Hal. I imagine we'll be seeing each other a lot now!" grinned Kevin and pedaled away, forcing Cathy to catch up to him.

"I never thought Hal liked me, too," said Cathy softly. "I'm so happy, Kevin, I can't even tell you! He is so ..."

"... so sweet, so nice, so wonderful, so sensitive, so unique, simply the nicest guy in the world. That's what

48

you want to say, isn't it?" Kevin completed her sentence, laughing, and Cathy gave him a look.

"That's right! How did you know?" she asked, astonished, not aware that Kevin was just teasing her.

"Intuition!" he answered with a deep voice and a mysterious tone.

"Intuition! You? You don't even know how to spell that word!" grinned Cathy, and then the two of them pedaled along in companionable silence.

The girl daydreamed about Hal and how their next meeting would go. Kevin, on the other hand, thought about Ricki and hoped that she was feeling better. A little cold wouldn't keep her down.

*

When they reached the Sulai farm, the stable was still brightly lit, and from the tack room window a light beamed out into the darkness.

"I wonder who's in there?" asked Kevin, more to himself than to Cathy, who also seemed a little surprised.

Quickly, they parked their bikes and walked into the stable.

"Hello, who's there?" called the boy. Since no one answered, he marched right into the tack room, where he found Lillian polishing her saddle with leather polish as though her life depended on it.

"Hi, how's Ricki?"

"She has a fever, and she's still asleep. Jake was in the house a while back and spoke with her mother."

"Oh, then it probably doesn't make any sense for me to go over there, does it?" Kevin sounded disappointed.

"No, probably not." Lillian looked up briefly, and only then did her friends notice that her eyes were very red and that she'd been crying.

Kevin and Cathy looked at each other with concern, and then slowly Cathy walked over to Lillian, sat down beside her, and put her arms around her.

"Josh?" was all she asked, and just speaking his name was enough to make Lillian start crying again.

Cathy felt almost guilty because she was so happy.

"Oh, come on, it'll straighten itself out," Cathy tried to comfort her, but Lillian was inconsolable.

"Nothing will work out!" she answered, sobbing so strongly that Cathy was startled. How could Lillian be so sure that it was over? After all, it hadn't been long ago that the two of them had been so great together.

"Why do you say that?"

"Because it's true!"

"Nonsense!"

Lillian blew her nose loudly. "I was out at the ranch, I wanted to see him and ... and Rebecca, too."

"Yeah? And did you?"

Lillian nodded.

"And?" Cathy asked again. "Go on, tell us!"

"Rebecca seems really nice. But she didn't have much time, because her mare was limping. Then I talked with Alex and he told me some things that Josh had said about me, things that are definitely not true!"

"I don't understand!"

"It doesn't matter. I already tried to tell you when we

50

were out riding. But whatever! Anyway, I was going to leave and then I bumped into Josh on the way out."

"Ah!"

"He acted so strange and was in such a hurry to see Rebecca ... and the good-bye he gave me was cool, to say the least."

Cathy and Kevin looked at each other sadly.

What could they say? Josh was a nice guy, and they all really liked him. At the moment they couldn't understand what was going on to make him treat Lillian this way.

"Do you think he's really interested in Rebecca?" asked Cathy. Lillian didn't answer. How could she? She didn't know herself.

Kevin looked down at Lillian and decided to talk to Josh about it in the next few days. Maybe she had just gotten all worked up about nothing and it wasn't as bad as it seemed. After all, girls always tended to be so dramatic.

"Anything new with you guys?" Lillian asked, trying to change the subject.

"Cathy likes Hal!" burst out Kevin. However, when he saw how Lillian reacted, he knew that he had said exactly the wrong thing.

"Thanks, Kevin!" Cathy snapped.

"It's okay," responded Lillian with a sad smile. "I'm really happy for you, Cathy. Does he like you, too?"

Cathy nodded.

"That's great! Enjoy this feeling as long as it lasts! You know, nothing is forever."

*

It was dark outside when Ricki woke up. Although there was no light by which to see, Ricki could just make out a tray on the table beside her bed, with a large mug of tea and a plate with tiny sandwiches and pieces of fruit under plastic wrap.

Slowly and with difficulty, Ricki sat up, glad that she could open her eyes, at least a little. Every movement hurt, and she couldn't remember ever being so sick that all of her joints ached like this.

Her mouth felt completely dry, and she reached a shaky hand toward the mug of tea. It felt as heavy as lead.

She drank a few sips before she put it back down, exhausted. Ricki was a little hungry, but the thought of chewing and swallowing was almost too much to bear.

Nevertheless, she remembered her mother's words, urging her to eat something, so she reached for a cheese sandwich. After she had taken one bite, she put it back down. Everything tasted like cardboard.

Wearily Ricki lay back down on her pillow. *What a mess!* she thought. She remembered that she'd wanted to ride over to Carlotta's with her friends. She wondered if they had gone without her.

Her thoughts were with Kevin, and she was disappointed that he hadn't shown up all afternoon.

Whatever, she thought, and sensed that she was falling asleep again.

*

It was relatively late when Carlotta came to visit Ricki's mother.

"I thought I'd better come by and see if everything's all

right," she said merrily, coming through the door. Of course she noticed that Brigitte wasn't in a good mood, but she ignored that.

"Would you have a cup of coffee for an old lady?" she asked, as she always did, when she came to visit.

"Yes, of course," replied Brigitte, although today she would have preferred not to have any more company.

"How's Ricki?" asked Carlotta directly when the two women were seated at the kitchen table.

"How did you know she's sick?"

"The jungle drums told me!" laughed Carlotta. "Kevin and Cathy were at my house today and they told me."

"Oh! I should have known." Brigitte now knew exactly why Carlotta had come by so late. Probably, she wanted to put in a good word for Ricki, and Diablo, too. It was always the same. Somehow, Brigitte always seemed to be alone with her viewpoint, and all of the others seemed to be against her if the topic was riding.

Carlotta was about to begin when Brigitte stopped her.

"Don't say anything! I know why you're here. I'm sure you've heard more horror stories about the evil mother who still thinks Ricki would be much safer without this horse!"

Carlotta looked at Brigitte thoughtfully. "I respect your opinion entirely, but ..."

"If you really do respect my opinion, then you can leave out your *but*!"

"No, I mean I just want to remind you that I was actually asking about Ricki."

"True. I'm sorry. She still has a fever and sleeps a lot."

"Fever? Did she catch something somewhere?"

"No, she went outside with soaking wet hair! In January! In below freezing temperatures! Imagine that!"

"Oh dear, sometimes kids just don't think about what they do," agreed Carlotta as she took a careful sip of hot coffee.

"See, and once again, she wouldn't have done it if it weren't for the horses! She had forgotten something in the stable and that's why she ran outside."

Carlotta rolled her eyes. "Yes, Brigitte, and if you had never met Marcus, Ricki would never have been born! Heavens, you always try to blame everything that happens to Ricki on the horses. I don't think that's fair!"

Brigitte stood up, very upset. "Let me tell you something. At the moment, I don't care if you think it's fair or not! After all, I'm the one who has to worry, not you! All you live for is your horses. They're like your children, and maybe you can understand me if I give you a similar example. How would you feel if you came into the stable one morning and discovered that one of your favorite horses was limping again? Assume that this happens often, and usually when a certain person has been riding him. Are you following?"

"Of course. Go on."

"What would you do in a case like this?"

Carlotta answered without hesitation. "I would punish that person."

"Exactly! And what would you do if the same thing kept happening?"

"I would probably throw that person out and never allow him or her in the stable again," admitted Carlotta, "but –"

"Now do you understand me? I'd like to throw out all of the horses so that nothing ever happens to Ricki again!" Brigitte's eyes sparkled.

Carlotta looked at her intensely. "You didn't let me finish. I wanted to say, however, that before I threw the person out, I would find out if that person was really to blame each time the horse started limping, or if it was possible that the horse had injured himself by doing something stupid!"

Brigitte's jaw muscles worked vigorously as Carlotta stood up to meet her eyes.

"Try to stay fair!"

"Thanks a lot! Jake said the same thing to me today."

"Well, then, maybe it's time for you to think it over. And now I'm going to leave, before you decide to throw me out as well! But if it's okay with you, I'd like to visit Ricki tomorrow," Carlotta said seriously, and Brigitte lowered her head.

"I'm sorry, Carlotta. I don't mean to be rude to you," she said softly. "But everyone always thinks I'm just against horses, and that's not true. I've always been afraid of the huge animals, and when I see Ricki coming home again and again with various injuries, I experience what happened to me as a child all over again."

Carlotta hesitated, and then she put her hands on Brigitte's shoulders and urged her down onto one of the chairs. Then she sat down again as well.

"Tell me what happened. How can you expect anyone to understand, if you never say what it is that really upsets you?"

"All right," Ricki's mother sighed and took a deep breath. "I was about seven years old, and in the small town where I grew up there was a brewery, which kept up the tradition of delivering their casks of beer in a wagon drawn by four enormous draft horses. For me, there was nothing more exciting than waiting at the edge of the road every Thursday to watch the wagon come around the corner. The driver would stop the wagon and let me sit on one of the animals and ride back to the brewery. One day I was sitting on one of the broad backed horses, when a truck came barreling around the corner headed directly toward us." Brigitte's eyes began to fill with tears as she recalled the event.

"This was the one time that they were so startled that they strained in their harnesses and bolted. I did my best to hold fast to the horse's mane, but it was impossible to stay on. At some point I slid off its back, down between the shaft and the horse, right past the thundering hooves. I was extremely lucky that I didn't get crushed under the wagon wheels. While I lay on the street, I saw a horrifying sight –the wagon had tipped over at the next corner and buried the driver. The animals kept on running until the straps broke. I don't know what happened to them because at the time I just stopped thinking."

Brigitte had turned pale, and she dabbed at her teary eyes with her handkerchief. Carlotta was finally able to understand why Ricki's mother had such a terrible fear of horses.

"What happened to the driver? Did he survive the accident?" she asked softly.

Brigitte shook her head. "No, unfortunately not, and with his death I lost the best grandfather a young child could hope to have."

"He was ... your grandfather?"

"Yes. And I will never forget how he died."

Chapter 4

Ricki woke the next morning feeling a little better. At least, she was hungry, and that told her that she was gradually getting better.

It must have been very early, because when Ricki opened her eyes, which she could finally do, thank heavens, everything was still in darkness.

Carefully, she felt for the lamp on her nightstand so that she wouldn't knock over her mug of tea, but when she turned it on nothing happened.

"Darn it!" Ricki growled. "The bulb's burned out!" She thought about getting up and turning on the ceiling light, but she decided to let it go. She just didn't feel like leaving her warm bed. Then she remembered that the plate with the sandwiches was still near her bed. She reached for it enthusiastically.

With every bite she felt better. She was consuming a delicious chicken salad sandwich when she heard the door open.

"Good morning, Ricki! How are you today? I'm so

glad you've got your appetite back!" Smiling, Brigitte approached her daughter's bed.

"Mom? What are you doing up so early?" Ricki asked, amazed.

Brigitte laughed. "Early? You're obviously still all mixed up. It's a beautiful winter day! The sun is shining from a blue sky, and for your information, it's already nine thirty."

Ricki froze. Slowly, she swallowed the last bit of bread. *Nine thirty?*

That can't be, droned through her head. *Mom's kidding. She's teasing me!*

"Could you ... could you please turn on the light?" Ricki pleaded, her voice shaking.

"Light? Why do you need light? It couldn't be any lighter than it already is in your room. I'm surprised you can sleep with so much light in here." Brigitte stood right in front of the bed. "What do you think? Can you get up for a minute so that I can fluff your pillow?"

Ricki stared straight ahead and didn't seem to take in what her mother was saying.

It's light in here! The words screamed in her head. *Why is she saying this? Oh, no. It's not light! Everything's dark! Black! Eternal night! Please, Mom, tell me that it's nighttime!*

"Ricki? Can you get up?" Brigitte asked once more, but then she looked at her daughter quizzically. "What's wrong with you?"

Slowly Ricki turned her eyes toward her mother, but somehow it seemed to Birgitta that her daughter was staring right through her. All of a sudden bitter tears began running down Ricki's cheeks.

"For heaven's sakes, honey, what's wrong? Tell me!" Brigitte sat down on the edge of the bed and took the weeping girl into her arms.

"Mom," Ricki whispered, barely audible. "Mom ... I can't ... see anything."

In that moment Brigitte thought that the floor would open up beneath her feet and swallow her. "What are you saying? I think I must have misunderstood you!"

"Everything ... everything is dark," Ricki repeated, pulling away, and then she began screaming at her mother in desperation. "All around me is darkness, do you understand me? I can't see! Mom, I'm blind! Please, Mommy, please make it so I can see again! Please ... please ... Mom ... ohhhh..." Ricki collapsed, sobbing, back into her mother's arms. She sobbed while her mother held her tightly, crying and staring at the ceiling.

Brigitte's thoughts were going around and around. *It can't be! What's happened? Somebody tell me it isn't true! It can't be! Ricki can't be blind! That's not possible.*

"Mom, please, help me!" she heard Ricki's pitiful voice, while the girl's hand felt over Brigitte's face. "Mom, please don't cry. You have to help me, somehow. You know everything. Please, Mom, please. I don't want to spend the rest of my life like this." Ricki grasped her mother and held on like someone drowning.

Brigitte didn't even hear her. The only thing she felt was her daughter's endless pain, and she was caught up in her panic.

"Ricki, sweetheart, don't be afraid. We'll fix this somehow," she whispered very softly. "We're going to get the doctor to come right away. I'm sure your blindness is ... a temporary condition. I'm sure that everything will be okay soon, and you'll be able to see again."

Ricki pressed herself tighter and tighter into Brigitte's arms. She forced her eyes open in the hope that she could see at least a glimmer of light, but everything remained clothed in darkness.

*

When Lillian, Cathy, and Kevin met at the bike stand in front of school, the boy whistled softly.

"Wow, Cathy, you're really looking good today!"

"Thanks for the compliment," responded Cathy, a slight pink glow lighting up her cheeks. "But does that mean that I usually don't look good?" she asked, laughing.

"You always look great, but today you look especially good! That's the power of love, I guess," he said, grinning.

"Love, and a little blusher!" Lillian corrected him, looking at Cathy with a knowing eye.

"You forgot the lip gloss!" Cathy said, and winked at her.

"Oh, you used makeup, well, then ..." Kevin ducked as Cathy swung her gym bag at him.

"Does anyone know how Ricki's doing?" Lillian asked.

Kevin turned to her. "If by 'anyone' you mean me, then I'd have to answer no. I don't know anything yet, either, but I think, judging by how she felt yesterday, that she won't be coming to school today. I wanted to call her this morning, but her mother would probably have killed me if the telephone had woken Ricki out of a healing sleep."

"You might be right about that." Lillian grabbed her backpack. "We'd better get going."

"Yeah, unfortunately!" sighed Cathy and thought once more of Hal. She wondered how she was ever going to survive the school day.

*

When the three friends split up inside the school, and Lillian had disappeared inside her classroom, Kevin turned to Cathy and said, "She seems to be dealing with the Josh situation better today than she did last night."

Cathy nodded. "Yeah, it looks like it. Still, I think it's really a huge shame that those two are breaking up."

"They haven't broken up yet!"

"But as good as, or do you see it differently?"

Kevin shrugged his shoulders. "At the moment all I see is Ms. Murphy, bearing down on us. If we don't hurry, we're going to get detention, and that's the last thing I need! Let's go!"

They started to run, and got to their seats just in time, before Ms. Murphy put her briefcase on the desk. Their teacher glared at the two friends, who looked back at her with innocent expressions on their faces.

"You two just made it," Ms. Murphy said with annoyance, and Kevin had to stop himself from making a joke.

*

Josh stood with Rebecca in front of Shakira's stall.

"Alex said it would be a miracle if I was able to start in

the show this weekend," Rebecca said, downcast. "What a mess! I'm an idiot. I should have been paying more attention when we were practicing."

"Oh, come on," Josh tried to console her. "Stuff like this can happen to anyone. You never know."

"Yeah, still, I feel like I'm to blame! After all, you all thought that I would be riding for the team on Shakira."

"Well, that's right, but I think it's more important that your sweet mare gets better. You can participate next time."

Rebecca gave him a grateful look. She really liked Josh; he was always so understanding.

"How come you're already here at the ranch this morning? Don't you have to work?" she asked him.

"No, I have the day off. We worked very late last night doing inventory. And why are you here?"

"I have two weeks of vacation."

"Vacation? What's that? I sure could use some of that."

Rebecca smiled. "You work for your father at the riding shop?"

"Yeah. I'm doing an apprenticeship as a retail salesman," explained Josh willingly. He appreciated Rebecca's interest.

"And? What's it like to have your father for your boss?" she asked.

Josh laughed. "Sometimes it's a pain, but there are advantages as well."

"For example?"

"Well, for example, if we're not busy he lets me leave early, and stays himself. If I were working somewhere else,

I'd have to stay and be bored. Of course, sometimes I have to stay late to go through the bills in the evening, but for the most part I have to admit, I have a pretty easy time at the shop."

Rebecca sighed. "You're so lucky. Slowly but surely I'm starting to regret that my parents don't have their own business. In the lawyer's office where I work, we never get to go home early. There's always one client after another, and we hardly have time to keep up with the correspondence because there's just so much to do."

"Oh, you poor thing! Then you've really earned your vacation!" Josh said with feeling.

"It's too bad Shakira can't be ridden, otherwise I'd have asked if you wanted to go riding," Rebecca said.

"Why don't I call Matt and ask him if you can ride his horse Ringo?" Josh suggested. "After all, the poor thing doesn't get enough exercise anyway. He's getting a big belly."

Rebecca's eyes beamed. Josh didn't even wait for her answer, but just grabbed his cell phone.

"This'll just take a few minutes!" he whispered to her as he strode toward the stable exit so that his cell phone could get better reception.

He was back in less than three minutes.

"Everything's settled. We can go! Matt said that if you can handle Ringo, he'll give you his place on the team, since you're a much better rider than he is."

"Really?" Rebecca was overjoyed, but she couldn't imagine that she would be able to achieve even half of what she could with Shakira.

"Yes!" Josh nodded vigorously. "Honestly, with Matt on the team and without your help, we wouldn't have a chance anyway."

"Well then, let's see how I make out with Ringo. Come on, let's go out on a trail ride so I can get used to him. Maybe I'll go to the riding hall afterward and do some test rounds," laughed Rebecca.

"That's great!" Josh was happy. The two of them got the horses ready to go riding.

*

After Ricki's desperation had turned into a silent apathy, her mother risked leaving her alone for a few minutes in order to make a few phone calls. She hated to do it, thinking of her daughter alone in her condition.

Thank goodness Harry isn't home, Brigitte thought as she dialed their doctor's number. She would need time to think about what to tell him about Ricki when he came home from school on the afternoon bus.

After several busy signals, she finally got through to the doctor's office and was connected to Dr. Leonard's receptionist.

"The doctor is busy with a patient right now," the nurse said a little stiffly. She wasn't pleased that Brigitte was insisting on speaking to the doctor personally.

"Listen closely to what I have to say. My daughter has gone blind over night, and I think that is a good enough reason to speak to Dr. Leonard personally for a few minutes on the phone. Is that too much to ask?"

Brigitte had to force herself to stay calm, but the nurse

had apparently understood that this was an emergency and connected her immediately to the doctor. She was soon comforted by the calm, reassuring voice of Dr. Leonard.

"Mrs. Sulai, hello. What did I just hear? Ricki can't see anything?"

Brigitte took a deep breath and explained the whole situation to the doctor. The doctor promised that he would come by the house within the next two hours.

"Of course, it would be better if you could bring Ricki to my office," he explained. "I have much better equipment here to examine her. Or you could drive her directly to an eye specialist; I will give you a referral."

"I would prefer it if you could take a look at her first. She had a fever last evening and during the night, and ..."

"All right, Mrs. Sulai. I'll come as soon as I can," Dr. Leonard promised Ricki's mother.

Then Brigitte tried to reach her husband at his office, but he wasn't there. He had just recently started working long hours on a new project and hadn't gotten home last night until late. Then he left early this morning, so she hadn't had a chance to tell him about Ricki. And now apparently he had gone to another site with clients and after that he intended to take them to dinner.

"Well, that's just terrific, Marcus. Just when I need you, you aren't available." Brigitte slammed the receiver down and tried to reach him on his cell phone, but he had switched it off.

Brigitte started toward Ricki's room, but then she ran back to the phone and dialed Carlotta's number.

"Mercy Ranch, Carlotta Mancini speaking," Carlotta answered crisply.

"Carlotta, it's me."

"Brigitte? What's up? You sound strange."

"I ... can you come over? I mean now? Immediately?"

Carlotta pressed the receiver to her ear because Brigitte's voice was becoming weaker and weaker. "I was just about to drive to the mill to order feed, because ..."

"It's about Ricki. She can't see!"

Carlotta stopped breathing for an instant. Completely shocked, she collapsed into her desk chair.

"Are you still there?" she heard Brigitte's voice coming from the receiver.

"Say that again. Ricki can't see? Why? What's happened?"

"I have no idea. She woke up this morning and ... can you come over?"

"I'm on my way. Don't panic, Brigitte! It's ... I'm sure it's temporary. See you in a few minutes!" Carlotta quickly put down the receiver and reached for her cane.

As fast as she could, she got going, and as she left the ranch house she called out to Kevin's mother, who took care of the household at Mercy Ranch, "Caroline, I'm going to the Sulais' and I have no idea when I'll be back. Could you please put some hay in the horses' racks at noon?"

Mrs. Thomas appeared in the doorway, laughing. "Yes, of course! Say hello to Brigitte and have a cup of coffee for me while you're there!"

Carlotta shook her head gravely. "I don't think we'll feel much like coffee today. Ricki can't see anything!"

Kevin's mother turned pale. She was about to interrogate Carlotta when the older woman raised her hand to stop her.

"Don't ask. I don't know the details. I'm on my way there now," Carlotta explained, and she got into her car and drove off with tires screeching.

"Ricki is blind? That's impossible! That just can't be!" Mrs. Thomas ran back into the kitchen completely shocked. She thought about her son. How would Kevin react to the news?

*

"Man, oh man, I'm so glad that school's over for the day!" Cathy took a deep breath as she stuffed the books that she had used in the last class into her backpack. "I thought I was going to fall asleep in history class. Ricki doesn't know how lucky she is that she missed this class today!"

Kevin slung his backpack over his shoulder.

"I don't know," he replied. "I think she'd rather be healthy and in school than sick in bed at home."

"You're right. Hey, are we getting together to go riding later this afternoon?" Cathy asked as they left the school building.

"Let's wait and see how the weather is. I definitely want to see Ricki, and I also need to groom Sharazan. Maybe I'll ride over to Carlotta's afterward. She'd probably be glad to have some help."

Cathy beamed. "That's a great idea! I'll come with you to the ranch."

Lillian, who had just joined them, smiled. "Hal is probably counting the hours until he sees you again, too."

"Do you think so?"

"Of course. He'd be crazy not to be thinking about you."

Kevin and Cathy were already seated on their bikes, waiting to ride home with Lillian.

"You two don't have to wait for me today. I'm going in the opposite direction."

Kevin looked at her, astonished. "How come? Where are you off to?"

"I want to ride out to the Western ranch. If I remember correctly, Josh told me that he's off today, and I assume that he'll be with Cherish. I'd like to try and talk to him again."

Cathy nodded. "Yeah. At least try. It's not completely over yet, is it? I'll keep my fingers crossed for you."

"Same here!" Kevin joined in. "Tell Josh to stop acting like a jerk. He should be glad he has a super girlfriend like you."

Lillian smiled gratefully at her friends. "You guys are really great. Thanks a lot. See you later this afternoon, okay? I'll be at the stable around three thirty."

"Okay, 'til then! And, Lillian, if he says any more stupid stuff, then just write it off to his being a man, okay?" Cathy called after her.

"Ho, ho, how funny!" Kevin stuck his tongue out at her.

"What's your problem? I didn't say anything against you," teased Cathy. "You aren't a man yet. You may become one, but at the moment ..."

"Enough!" Kevin scooped up a handful of snow and threw it at Cathy.

"Snowball fights are forbidden on school property!

Kevin! Cathy! Come here ..." Ms. Murphy's voice rang out across the schoolyard.

"Oh, man, let's get out of here!"

Immediately the two of them rode off on their bikes before their teacher could call them again.

*

"That wasn't bad at all," declared Josh, after Rebecca had ridden the course on Ringo in the hall.

"It wasn't bad, but it wasn't good enough to win any prizes at the show," replied Rebecca. "It's easy to see that Matt hasn't worked with his horse at all in the last few weeks. Ringo just needs a little more training."

Josh nodded. He thought exactly the same thing.

"That's enough for today. We don't want the poor animal to get a charley horse!" laughed Rebecca, giving Josh hot and cold shivers all along his back. He had loved that laugh since the first time he heard it.

He quickly came down from the stands and opened the ropes gallantly so that Rebecca could leave the arena with Ringo and lead him to his stall.

While she took care of Matt's horse, Josh watched her every move, and all of a sudden Rebecca seemed to notice his glance. Slowly she turned to him and looked deeply into his eyes.

"Your girlfriend was at the stable yesterday," she said.

"Yeah, I know. I ran into her at the door," Josh replied, a little unnerved.

Rebecca tilted her head to one side. "She seemed really nice."

"You think so?"

"Yes. But when I look at you right now, I can't dismiss the feeling that your relationship isn't doing so well lately. How come?"

"Well," he said slowly, "you're right. Lillian really is sweet, but our riding interests are completely at odds, and so we get into lots of arguments. Western-style riders and English style don't really get along very well."

Rebecca looked at him intensely. "That can't be the problem, can it?"

Josh's face turned red. "You're right," he admitted. "That's not really the reason."

"That's what I thought. Do you want to tell me what's going on? I mean, you don't have to, but ..."

"It's okay." Josh gathered his courage and looked straight at Rebecca. "It's like this. I think I've fallen for someone else."

"Oh. Who's the lucky person?"

Josh took a deep breath, and his heart was racing.

"You," he said quietly.

Rebecca swallowed. "Me? You're not serious?"

"Yes, I am, Becky."

They looked at each other in silence for a long time. Then the young woman put her arms around Josh's neck and tousled his hair affectionately.

"Josh, your feelings for me mean a lot to me," she responded. "I've been noticing it for quite a while, but I thought I was mistaken."

While Rebecca and Josh were engaged in conversation, Lillian entered the stables full of hope that she and Josh could clear up their misunderstanding with a talk. However, when she saw her boyfriend in front of Ringo's stall with Rebecca's arms around his neck, she stood stock-still. Tears of disappointment and rage filled her eyes, and she balled her hands into fists.

She would have liked to run over to them and slap *her* Josh in the face, but she couldn't get up enough courage in her anger.

Her Josh ... He would never be *her* Josh again! That much was clear. She had seen enough!

She turned away quickly and left the stable unnoticed. She was sure that she would never forget the image of Rebecca with her arms around Josh.

You jerk! thought Lillian, pedaling away furiously on her bike. It wasn't even clear in her mind at that moment whether she meant Josh or Rebecca – or herself. However, she was positive that she never wanted to see Josh again.

Chapter 5

Carlotta didn't reach the Sulai farm until two hours later, just as Dr. Leonard was on his way back to his office. With difficulty, she maneuvered herself out of her car and slumped straight into Jake's arms.

"What happened to you?" the elderly stable hand asked and pointed to spots of dirt that dotted Carlotta's light-colored jacket.

"I had a flat tire and, unfortunately, also a defective spare tire in the trunk. I'd forgotten to have it repaired after driving over a nail two months ago. It was total chaos until I finally found a garage where I could get a new tire."

"Don't you know you shouldn't drive around without a functioning spare tire?" Jake asked.

"Of course I know that, but there are more important things in life. How is she?"

"How am I? Thanks, I'm fine. A little back pain ..."

"Not you! Ricki!"

"Ricki? I have no idea. Last night she still had a fever,

but I haven't been over to the house yet this morning. I was just on my way there to see how she is."

Carlotta paused, perplexed. "So you don't know yet?" she asked.

"What don't I know?"

"Brigitte called me this morning. Ricki can't see!"

"WHAT?!" Jake turned pale. "Why? I mean, yesterday she was okay. Why didn't anyone tell me? I would have ... Ah well, no one tells me anything anymore. I'm beginning to wonder if I still exist!"

"Jake, don't get all worked up. This isn't the time to feel sorry for yourself. I imagine Brigitte had other things on her mind than looking for you somewhere in the stable!"

"She knows exactly where to find me. No one has to go looking for me," grumbled the old man, hurt. Then he followed behind Carlotta, who was already on her way to the house.

Before the two of them entered the house, they exchanged a worried look, then they gathered their courage and Carlotta opened the door.

"Brigitte?" she called quietly. "I'm here."

Listening, she stayed down at the bottom of the stairs, but when no one appeared she decided to go up to Ricki's room.

On the middle of the stairs, she saw Rosie, Ricki's dog, coming toward her. After a little growling, Rosie recognized Carlotta and wagged her tail.

"Well, my dear, let's go to Ricki's room," coaxed Carlotta.

"Oh, here you are, finally," Brigitte said, standing in Ricki's doorway. She looked exhausted and her eyes were red from crying.

"Sorry it took me so long to get here. Flat tire," Carlotta explained brusquely, and Jake, who was upset with Ricki's mother because she hadn't told him about the girl's condition, felt a heaviness in his heart when he saw Brigitte.

"How is she?" he asked, his voice shaking.

Ricki's mother closed the door softly behind her. "Dr. Leonard was just here and he examined her," she whispered.

"And? What did he say?"

"Well, it isn't that simple. There are several factors to consider. The way I see it, he didn't really know himself, exactly."

"Come on, tell us!" Carlotta was becoming more anxious the longer Brigitte took to answer them.

"First of all, he said that she has a serious case of the flu. But we'd seen that yesterday, when she was running a high fever. It had to happen, after her foolishness of going outside with soaking wet hair in zero-degree weather! Anyway, as far as this sudden blindness is concerned, he thinks it's possible that the branch that whipped across Ricki's eyes with such force may have caused some sort of trauma – the object smashing into her, the contusion and swelling, mixed with a bad headache brought on by the flu, add to that the fever – it may have all contributed to the blindness. At least that's what I understood him to say. He can't be sure."

"Isn't there anything that can be done? I mean, with an operation or with lasers or whatever."

"Dr. Leonard said he thinks they may heal on their own but he didn't want to make any promises. He wants me to take Ricki to the eye clinic today to see a specialist. We have an appointment for this afternoon. I hope Ricki will feel better by then. She was so upset that her fever rose again."

"It's good that you're going to see an eye specialist today," replied Carlotta. "I hope it turns out to be as Dr. Leonard suspected. I can certainly understand Ricki's frustration. I would go crazy if I were in her situation."

"Me too," admitted Brigitte. "But if the blindness has another cause, then, of course, it will be a completely different situation," she added softly.

Jake cleared his throat. "May I visit her for a few minutes?" he asked quietly.

Brigitte nodded.

"Thank you." With his heart beating fiercely, he opened the door carefully. Entering the room without a sound, he saw the teenager lying still on her bed, her eyes wide open, staring at the ceiling. Just her hands were moving, nervously gliding back and forth on the blanket.

"Ricki?" Softly, Jake spoke to her, but beyond a slight tremor he couldn't tell whether she had heard him or not.

"Ricki, I wanted to say hello from ... from Diablo, and he wants you to hurry up and get well again so that you can brush his coat."

What kind of nonsense am I talking here? the old man scolded himself as he watched the girl closely.

"I already cleaned out his hooves this morning, and I think he's going to need new shoes soon. Did you notice that, too?"

Ricki swallowed, and Jake had the impression that she

wanted to say something, but no sound was coming from her lips, even though she moved them slightly.

"Oh yeah, and I saw that your saddle got pretty wet yesterday. You know that makes spots on the leather. You should rub in more saddle conditioner so that the dampness won't damage the leather. You might be able to do that in the next few days, don't you think?" If Ricki didn't answer him soon, Jake wouldn't be able to think of anything more to say. He was too distressed to mention anything about her eyes.

"Jake," Ricki whispered, "Jake, I ... I can't see anything."

Jake brushed away his tears. "I know, child."

Ricki turned to him, but she stared past his face as she stretched out her trembling hands toward him. He grabbed them and held them tight.

"Do you know what that means?"

Jake nodded, forgetting that Ricki couldn't see him.

"I'll never again be able to watch Diablo gallop across the paddock. I'll never be able to look at his wonderful head, never see him looking at me when I come into the stable ... never be able to ride again, never see the sun again, my friends, my family. Jake, I can't spend the rest of my life in darkness."

Jake sat down on the edge of the bed and stroked her cheek awkwardly.

"You won't have to," he said hoarsely and tried to make his voice sound convincing. Nevertheless, Ricki noticed that his voice was quivering slightly.

"The doctor says ..."

"I know what the doctor said, but my gut tells me

something different, and you know that I have always been able to trust my gut feelings up to now." Ricki tightened her grip on Jake's hands.

"Jake, tell me, what did I do wrong?" Tears filled Ricki's eyes and rolled down her cheeks until they were soaked up by her pillow.

"You didn't do anything wrong, Ricki Sulai! And if I tell you that you're going to see again, then that's the way it will be!"

Jake felt so helpless. He had an urge to run out of the crowded little room, out into an open field, to breathe the fresh air. His worries for Ricki were almost suffocating him.

"Carlotta is here. Should I call her?" he asked.

"Whatever," Ricki said indifferently. She didn't care whether anyone visited her or not. The only one she would have wanted to visit her was Kevin, but she didn't dare think about how he would react when he found out that he had a girlfriend who was blind.

"Okay, child, I'm going to leave now. The horses are probably hungry. It's already way past noon. Carlotta will be right in." Jake got up awkwardly and regarded the girl with a look full of pain. Gently he removed his hand from hers. She had held on tightly the whole time he had been with her.

"Don't give up, Ricki! I know you're going to make it," he whispered to her. He had to leave. He couldn't stand seeing Ricki in this condition any longer.

Jake went downstairs to find Carlotta. "She's expecting you. She's convinced her blindness is permanent, and frankly, I don't have a very good feeling about this either!"

78

he blurted out as he hurried out of the house and fled to the stable, where he cried his eyes out on Diablo's neck. Ricki, whom he loved like a granddaughter, just couldn't go blind!

*

Carlotta's visit with Ricki wasn't much different from Jake's, other than the fact that she had herself under more control and even managed to make her voice sound almost normal in Ricki's presence.

"There's no sense losing hope, my dear," she said. "That won't help the situation at all. If you want to get better, then you have to do something, too. It does no good to lie here and just accept the fact that you're blind. You have to start right now to think differently about it."

"But I feel that ..." the girl tried to object.

Carlotta refused to listen. "Your feelings! You know, Ricki, that I have always trusted your feelings. Nevertheless, it is often the case that you can be mistaken about your feelings when you're the one involved. That's why I refuse to listen to your gut feeling in this case, and would rather pay attention to the way I feel! And I am convinced that you will see again!"

"I really, really hope so," answered Ricki softly and closed her eyes. The conversation had taken a lot out of her.

"Don't hope so or wish it were so. *Know* that it will be so," Carlotta said passionately, and then she said good-bye quietly and left the room with Brigitte, who had been standing in the doorway and had heard everything.

"Now a cup of coffee would really do me some good," she said, exhausted, as Brigitte took her in her arms.

"And you're going to have a cup! Thank you, Carlotta! I'm so glad you're here!"

*

Kevin had just arrived home and was warming up some leftover spaghetti when the phone rang.

"Yeah," he answered abruptly while he licked the spoon he'd used to stir the sauce.

"Kevin, it's good you're home!"

"Hi, Mom, what's up? Did Gandalf break loose again?" The boy pictured himself out looking for his dog again. During the day his mother always took the dog with her to Mercy Ranch.

"No! Sit down for a moment and listen to me!"

"What's wrong? You sound so weird! Wait a minute!" Kevin turned off the stove and removed the pot from the hot burner. Then he went into the living room to lie down and relax on the sofa. "Tell me. Nothing will bother me now," he said laughing.

He shot straight up when he heard the news about Ricki. "Say that again! And please, tell me it's not true!"

"Honey, I'm so sorry, but that's what Carlotta told me before she drove off for the Sulai farm, and that was almost three hours ago."

"That's impossible!" Kevin felt dizzy all of a sudden. "I ... I'll get going right away. I don't know when I'll be back home!" Without waiting for his mother's response, he ended the call and let the receiver drop. He felt as though someone had punched him in the stomach.

Ricki, he thought in disbelief. *My Ricki!* He couldn't

think of anything else. It was simply impossible for him to imagine that his girlfriend couldn't see.

"I've got to call Cathy and Lillian," he mumbled to himself, startled by his own voice. It sounded so strange.

*

Cathy was as upset as Kevin about the news concerning Ricki. While he was on his way to his girlfriend, she tried to reach Lillian. After the fourth try, she gave up and decided to go over to her house. She was sure Lillian would be back from the Western ranch by now.

"Have you done your homework?" Mrs. Sutherland asked. Cathy had been home only an hour, and now she was putting on her jacket and saying good-bye again.

"No, not yet, but ..."

"Then do that first, please! Rashid will be okay if you do your schoolwork first."

"Mom, you don't understand! It's not about Rashid! It's about Ricki. She ..."

"She can wait, too!" replied Mrs. Sutherland, unmoved.

"Mom, at least listen to me! She ..."

"No! You listen! You aren't going anywhere until you have finished your homework! Do you understand me?" With these words, Cathy's mother turned around and disappeared into the kitchen.

The girl stomped her foot in frustration. Why wouldn't her mother ever listen to her?

For a moment, Cathy stood in the hallway, undecided. Then she zipped up her parka and stormed out of the house. Nothing was going to stop her from riding to her friend's house. Cathy just had to know what the situation was concerning Ricki.

When the door slammed shut, Mrs. Sutherland looked out the window and could just see Cathy as she got on her bike and rode off as fast as she could.

"That is unbelievable!" she murmured, furiously. "Just wait till you get home this evening, young lady!"

*

Lillian heard her cell phone ringing. She could tell from the caller ID number that Cathy was trying to reach her, but she didn't feel like talking to anyone just now.

When she finally arrived back home, she had greeted her parents somewhat rudely, and then gone straight to her room. She didn't intend to leave it anymore today. Holli would have to do without her for one day.

*

Brigitte had been getting up and looking in on Ricki every few minutes until Carlotta stopped her.

"You're not doing her a favor by going in there all the time, Brigitte. Give her a chance to rest. How can she do that if you keep going into her room?"

"But what if she needs something or has to go to the bathroom?"

"Then she can call you. Believe me, she needs a little time to herself so that she can deal with this."

"But ..."

Carlotta pushed Brigitte back into her chair.

"Trust me, I know what I'm talking about. When my daughter, Sarah, was struggling with her cancer, I thought

I had to be with her all the time, but then she told me very clearly how important it was for her to have some time alone to herself."

"But people are different."

"Yes, they are, but ..."

Brigitte sighed. "Okay, Carlotta. I get it."

"Good! Give her at least an hour to herself before you go in again. Have you been able to reach Marcus yet?"

Brigitte shook her head. "No. Everything's going wrong today," she responded, and poured Carlotta another cup of coffee. "Be honest. Do you really believe that Ricki will be able to see again?" she asked after a while.

Her older friend looked at her silently for a long while before she answered. "I don't know, Brigitte, but the doctor gave you hope, at least, and that means that he thinks the chances are good."

"But what if he's wrong? Do you think Ricki would be able to deal with not being able to see?"

"Hmm, in this case, she wouldn't have any alternative, but let's not think about that now. There's plenty of time for that if the situation actually occurs."

"But ..."

"Brigitte, stop it! I can easily imagine what's going through your mind, but you should try to direct your thoughts toward Ricki's health. That's the only way you can be of help to her!"

Ricki's mother nodded silently. She knew Carlotta was right, but she couldn't change the way she felt. The fear she felt for her daughter was tearing her apart.

Cathy finally reached the Bates farm. She leaned her bike carelessly against the side of the house before she began ringing the doorbell.

"Hello, Cathy. Lillian is upstairs in her room," she heard someone calling out of the stable window.

"Hey, thanks, Mrs. Bates. I'll go on up. Oh, goodness, Mowgli, look at you! Were you rolling in the mud?" She tried in vain to get away from Lillian's dog, who was giving her a frisky greeting. The dog kept jumping up on her and trying to lick her face. "Oh, no! Now look what you did! Aren't you ashamed of yourself?" Cathy kept him away from her as much as she could, but only when Mrs. Bates called, "Here, Mowgli," did the dog let her go and then, insulted, he trotted off toward the stalls.

"Thanks!" Cathy called to Lillian's mother as she entered the house. "Lillian ... LILLIAN, are you upstairs?" She quickly took off her shoes, ran upstairs in her socks, and pushed open her girlfriend's door.

"Are you crazy? You scared me to death!" Lillian was lying in bed and now she put her pillow over her face. "I'm not going to the stable today," she said.

"Did you turn your cell phone off? Why didn't you answer when I called?" Cathy asked as she pulled the pillow from Lillian's head.

"Hey, what are you doing? Leave me alone!"

"Come on, get up, we have to go over to Ricki's house!"

"I just said that I'm not going to the stable today. Didn't you ...?"

"I didn't say anything about going to the stable. We have to go visit Ricki. She can't see!" Cathy burst out finally. Lillian looked at her dumbfounded.

"Are you out of your mind? Why do you think she can't see?"

"I have no idea! Kevin called me a while ago and told me. He's probably there already. I couldn't reach you, unfortunately!"

"What? Are you serious?" Lillian jumped out of bed, now wide-awake.

"Yes!"

"So why are we still here? Come on, let's go!" Lillian grabbed Cathy's hand and pulled her along. If what she had just told her were true, then they couldn't afford to waste any time. Ricki probably felt alone, and would be glad to have her friends around her.

I'm lying here feeling sorry for myself because Josh has another girlfriend, and poor Ricki's feeling much, much worse, Lillian thought, angry with herself for ignoring Cathy's call. If she'd answered the phone, she would already be with her friend.

"Hurry up," she urged Cathy, who was struggling with her wet shoelaces. The knots were covered with ice.

"Just a minute. I can't perform magic!" Finally, Cathy managed to tie her shoes and the two girls were on their way to the neighboring Sulai farm, riding their bikes on the narrow winter road as fast as they could.

Kevin was already on his way to Ricki's room.

Chapter 6

Brigitte's frequent visits to her daughter's room – all that
hovering – irritated Ricki. Just the fact that she couldn't
see who was coming into her room completely unnerved
her. And the thought that her blindness might become
permanent made her almost crazy.

Why? she kept asking herself. *Why me?*

Ricki's emotions went from rage to helplessness to
bottomless sadness. But when she remembered what
Carlotta had said to her, she stiffened her resolve. She
would not give up! She would fight her blindness and win,
no matter what it cost her ... and yet, what if the doctor was
wrong? What if he had given her false hope just to calm her
down until she had gotten used to the condition?

Her thoughts were swirling around in her head and she
felt uncertain about everything. All she wanted to do was
sleep and then wake up to find out that all of this was just a
bad dream. Then she would get up, take a cold shower, and
go over to the stable to see Diablo. She would groom him,

saddle him, and then go for the most beautiful winter ride through the countryside.

Diablo ...

Ricki's heart pained her at the thought of her darling horse. What would become of him if she were permanently blind? Would Jake be able to take care of him? After all, he wasn't young anymore. Would her parents sell her horse if she couldn't ride him anymore?

Ricki was becoming panicky.

Maybe Kevin could take care of Diablo.

She sighed deeply.

Kevin ...

She wished he were here beside her, and yet she was afraid of how he would react to her condition.

I wonder if he will stay with me even though I can't see, the girl asked herself for the hundredth time.

Ricki was so sad. If she lost Kevin, too, her life would never be the same.

*

Someone was knocking timidly on her door, and then Ricki heard the door open quietly.

"Mom, please. I want to be alone," Ricki said softly.

"Hello, Ricki. It's me."

"Kevin!" Ricki's voice threatened to give way. At the moment she didn't know whether to be happy or sad that her boyfriend had come. On the one hand, she was overjoyed by his visit, but on the other, the next few minutes would probably let her know if he was going to be able to deal with her problem.

"How are you?" The boy had hardly spoken these words when he realized that that was probably the dumbest question ever, given the situation.

Ricki tried a smile and turned her head in the direction where she thought her boyfriend was.

"Well, not so hot," she said haltingly and felt very close to tears.

Kevin sat down on the chair next to her bed, took her hand, swallowed hard, and could think of nothing to say. If only he knew what to do. Normally he had no problem talking to Ricki for hours on end, but today everything seemed different.

"Kevin, I don't know if I will ever see again," Ricki broke the silence. She had to say it, right away, before Kevin tried to steer the conversation in another direction.

"I heard. Your mother and Carlotta told me," he replied softly.

Ricki turned her head to the side and bit her lip. "And you came anyway?"

"Of course. Why wouldn't I?" Kevin's heart throbbed painfully. "Nothing's changed between us."

Ricki shrugged her shoulders. "I thought maybe you ... I mean ..." she stammered. She simply couldn't say what she had been thinking.

"Did you think that maybe I would just walk away?"

"No, but I was afraid you wouldn't be able to deal with the fact that I can't see."

"How could you think that of me? You know me better than that. And anyway, your mother told me the doctor thinks that in time you'll be able to see again. Carlotta is convinced of that as well."

"Everybody seems to be convinced of it but me," Ricki said.

"But that's the most important thing of all. You have to believe in yourself."

"It sounds as though you've all talked it over beforehand. Why won't someone just tell me exactly what the situation really is?"

"That's what we're doing, but you don't seem to want to believe us!"

"It's easy for you to say! Just try to put yourself in my shoes. Wouldn't you lose hope if everything around you was black?"

Kevin was silent.

He understood how Ricki could feel that way. He understood her fear, or at least he thought he did. But that was what she couldn't imagine. How could he understand how she felt, when he could see all of the wonderful colors that surrounded him?

Ricki didn't say anything more, either, and they experienced an embarrassing silence between them that they'd never known before.

"I'm sure you're tired and want to sleep now," Kevin said after a few minutes.

"Yeah, you're right," Ricki whispered in a sad voice. She wasn't tired, but she didn't want to force Kevin to stay there and hold her hand out of pity.

"Will you come back?" she asked.

"Of course!" the boy promised, and he bent over her

and kissed her gently on the forehead. "Don't worry, Ricki, everything's going to be all right."

Ricki didn't answer. She heard Kevin tiptoe quietly toward the door.

"I hope so," she said softly after Kevin had left the room. Then she allowed herself to feel the awful loneliness that was pressing against her heart, and she sobbed bitterly.

*

"I think it would be better if you visited Ricki tomorrow," Brigitte said to Lillian and Cathy, who were staring apprehensively at an ashen-faced Kevin just as he came down the stairs.

"Hey, Kevin, how is she?"

"She's not in a good mood, but how could she be?" Helplessly, he looked at Carlotta, who put her arm around him to comfort him.

"She needs you now more than ever," she said to him, not realizing what a heavy burden this placed on his shoulders.

Kevin nodded. "I know, but I have no idea if I'll be able to help her."

"Just knowing that you're there for her will give her strength and hope."

"Do you think so?"

"Yes, but only if she believes that you're sincere and honest." Carlotta looked directly into his eyes.

"Carlotta, please!" Brigitte tried to silence her friend, but Carlotta just ignored her.

"The healing power of hope is very strong. If Ricki can

put her trust in her friends, then there's a very good chance she'll make it."

"Do you really think so? She thinks that no one is telling her the truth. For her, it seems clear that she's going to stay blind." Kevin's voice shook.

"At the moment she's just sick and desperately unhappy. We all have to keep her spirits up and convince her that the opposite is true. Hopefully, one of the doctors at the clinic will tell her that she's going to be okay."

Ricki's mother nodded in agreement.

"Maybe we should go to the horses," said Kevin, lowering his gaze. He really needed to get himself together. "I have to untangle Sharazan's tail," he mumbled.

"It's okay, Kevin," Carlotta said. "We're all overwhelmed by this event. Give Rashid a carrot for me, okay?"

Kevin said nothing more. He just nodded and left the house.

With heavy hearts, Cathy and Lillian watched him leave, and then they followed after him. Secretly, they were relieved that they weren't going to see Ricki until tomorrow. Neither of them felt prepared to deal with their friend's condition.

*

Josh sat on a chair in his father's riding shop. He had volunteered to give up the rest of his day off to wait on customers for the last four hours they were open.

"Well, son, what's the matter with you today?" Josh's father asked, "This isn't like you at all."

Josh said nothing as he busied himself with mindless

activities around the store. There were few customers today, and the distraction Josh had hoped for of working in the shop didn't happen. He had even more time for soul searching than he wanted.

He kept seeing Rebecca in front of him, feeling her hands on his shoulders and hearing her words after he'd told her that he was crazy about her.

"Josh, I'm touched by your interest, really. I've noticed something for quite some time, but I thought I must be wrong. You're a really nice guy, and I could imagine having more feelings for you than just friendship, if ... well, if it weren't for the fact that I already have a boyfriend. We've been together for over two years and we're as happy together as we were in the beginning. I would never do anything to jeopardize our relationship. It means too much to me. I hope you can accept that."

Josh felt like a fool. He should have known that someone as nice as Rebecca would already have a boyfriend.

"And what about Lillian, your girlfriend? She is so sweet, and you two suit each other really well. Alex told me the story of your experience with the rowboat on Echo Lake, and that you've always been so happy together until recently. Tell me, Josh, am I the reason you two aren't getting along? That would be awful!"

Josh had no answer for her. He just said good-bye and left quickly. He couldn't stand to be around her any longer.

Now he was staring at the shelf where the brushes and grooming equipment were stacked and trying to sort things out. He'd really acted like an idiot at the ranch today. What would Rebecca think of him the next time they ran into one another? He especially dreaded the looks he knew he would get from his buddies. Rebecca would certainly tell them about his declaration of affection.

All of a sudden everything was totally clear, and he slapped his palm against his forehead.

"How can I have been such a jerk?" he asked himself, and suddenly he saw Lillian in his mind's eye, heard her wonderful laugh, how she embraced Holli so lovingly, and also, how she bent down to give him a kiss.

I am an incredible jerk, he scolded himself. *I must have been completely crazy to chase after a dream, when I already have one of the sweetest girls imaginable for my girlfriend. Rebecca was right!*

Suddenly Josh realized how stupidly he'd been behaving toward Lillian the last few weeks, and he felt guilty. And he was afraid that Lillian had noticed his interest in Rebecca.

"I hope not, otherwise my chances are not good," he murmured to himself. Then he stood up abruptly and called out to his father.

"Dad, can I go?" he asked, a little embarrassed.

"That sure was a short-term offer to work," his father laughed. "Yes, you can go, but you'll have to make up the time tomorrow."

"Okay! Bye, boss! I'm going to ride over to Lily's!"

"That's what I thought. Say hello to her for me. By the way, the new snaffle she ordered a few days ago has delivery problems."

"Okay, I'll tell her!" Josh was out the door in one leap.

He couldn't wait to get into his old car and drive to the Bates farm. He was sure Lillian would be pleased if he picked her up and invited her out for dessert at her favorite restaurant.

*

The friends stood silent and downcast as they groomed their horses. The girls were looking at Kevin, who kept his back to them so they couldn't see how upset he was. With patience and devotion, he combed Sharazan's tail.

Lillian could hardly stand the silence. She found it terrible watching Kevin suffer.

Spontaneously, she threw her currycomb aside and went over to the boy and put her arm around him. She didn't say anything.

Kevin stopped what he was doing and starred at the roan's croup.

"I'm okay," he said quietly. "Really."

"Well, then, everything's okay," replied Lillian. She sensed that Kevin found her hug unwelcome. Apparently, he wanted to be alone with his feelings. The sixteen-year-old immediately took a step backward.

"Thanks," whispered Kevin. Then he leaned against his horse and his shoulders began to shake.

"Poor Ricki," he stammered as tears rolled down his cheeks. "She can't stay blind! She just can't!"

Cathy and Lillian looked helplessly at one another. They felt the same pain in their hearts Kevin did, but as they hadn't yet seen Ricki, it was easier for them to stay calm.

"Ricki asked me if I could deal with her being blind, and honestly I ... I don't know if I can. I feel so ... so helpless."

Kevin's eyes wandered around the stable and settled on Diablo. "He's going to miss her the most."

Cathy swallowed hard. "I'm sure she's going to be able to see again!"

"And if she can't?"

"Don't think like that, Kevin. Carlotta said ..."

"Oh, come on, Carlotta is just trying to console us," Kevin said more harshly than he'd intended.

"Does that mean you don't believe Ricki's going to get better?" Lillian stared at him in shock.

"I don't know what I believe anymore. Right now, all I'm sure of is the feeling of emptiness inside me.

Cathy put aside her grooming equipment. "Want to take the horses out for a ride?"

"Not now. I definitely don't feel like riding," Kevin said emphatically.

"Oh, come on, Kevin. There's no point in our just hanging around here and not talking to each other. Regardless of how we feel, the horses need some exercise. Ricki would want us to look after them. And I think it would do us good to get some fresh air," Lillian responded.

"Why don't the two of you go by yourselves?"

"Because we just wouldn't feel right leaving you here alone."

Kevin didn't say anything. He gathered up his grooming tools, went to the tack room, and came back with his saddle over his arm.

"All right," he said softly. "Let's go, but let's take Diablo with us on a lead."

Lillian breathed a sigh of relief. "Okay! Come on, Cathy, let's hurry before Kevin changes his mind."

*

Ricki could hear the soft voices of her friends beneath her window, but she couldn't make out what they were saying.

Cathy and Lillian had come, but they hadn't thought it necessary to stop by and see her even for a few minutes.

That's the way it is with friends, Ricki thought bitterly. *You're of interest to them only when you don't have any problems. Some friends! I always thought those two were different, but apparently I was wrong. And Kevin will stop coming, too. I just know it!*

Suddenly she heard a horse neighing that she would have known anywhere. Her head shot up.

"Diablo!" she whispered and listened attentively.

"All set?" she heard Kevin shouting. She realized that her friends were going riding and were going to take Diablo on a lead.

It hurt Ricki terribly that life seemed to be going on as usual. But what did she expect? That everyone would gather around her bed and feel sorry for her?

Well, at least they were considerate enough to take her darling horse with them on their ride so he would get some exercise, too. Hadn't that been her wish? That Kevin would take care of Diablo?

Ricki had the uncontrollable desire to see her horse, or at least to feel him close to her. She pushed the blanket aside and felt for her slippers with her feet, but she couldn't find them.

She felt bitterness rising within her. If she couldn't manage to find even the simplest things in her own room, how was she ever going to deal with life on the outside?

She could have wept, not out of self-pity but out of the anger that was growing inside her.

All of a sudden, though, the slippers were no longer important.

Ricki stood up and tried to remember if she had left anything lying on the floor yesterday that she might stumble over now, but she couldn't think of anything. She imagined it was nighttime and that she was trying to go to the window and open it without turning on the light, something that she did quite often.

With her hands stretched out in front of her, she walked across her room on wobbly legs. If she was remembering it correctly, she would soon be near the chair that was in front of the little table, where she often banged her knee.

Ricki bent down and moved her hands around so that she could feel the furniture, but she couldn't find anything in her reach.

"Where's that stupid chair?" The girl pressed her lips together and took tiny steps because she was afraid that any minute now she would bump into something.

"Okay, Jake, see you later. We won't be gone long," she heard Cathy, outside.

"Darn it!" Ricki turned completely around. She had lost her orientation because the voice was coming from a different direction.

She kept going, cautiously, and then, nevertheless, she banged hard against the edge of her desk.

"Ouch!" she burst out. She pressed her hand on her thigh, which was probably going to be black and blue tomorrow. But at least now she knew where she was. Slowly, she moved around the desk and felt for the curtains, which had been pulled to the side.

She felt for the window and pushed it wide open.

"Take care of Diablo!" she called out loudly, not knowing if her friends were even still nearby.

The three friends turned around abruptly and, startled, stared up at her.

The girl leaned far out of the window in order to hear at least something.

"For heaven's sake, Ricki. Take a step back," shouted Kevin. "Are you crazy? What are you doing at the window? Close it!"

They were still there!

"Are you going to take him on a lead, Kevin?"

"Yeah. Did you hear me? I asked you to close the window," she heard Kevin urging her again.

What am I, a little kid? Ricki asked herself and in that instant she felt like an idiot.

"I'm being careful!" she responded petulantly. "It's not the first time I've stood at my window!"

"But you're forgetting that you're bli ..." Kevin clapped his hand over his mouth.

Ricki froze. "As if I could ever forget that," she said softly and sadly, and then took a step backward and closed the window.

She heard the door to her bedroom open and then her mother yelling.

"Ricki! What are you doing there? You can't just ... you weren't at the window, I hope?"

The girl let her head hang.

Did being blind mean that you weren't allowed to do anything you used to do all the time?

"I just wanted to know ..."

"Promise me you will never open this window! At the moment, it's just too dangerous for you," Brigitte said anxiously.

"But if I can't see anything anymore, then, at least I want to breathe in the life that's going on around me. I want to hear Diablo moving through the snow, Mom, can't you understand that?"

Brigitte swallowed. Of course she could understand her daughter, but the fear that something else might happen to her gripped her.

"You're going to be able to see Diablo soon, but until then, Ricki, I'm begging you to be reasonable and careful."

"Reasonable?" The girl's voice shook. She hated that word! "I can't lie in bed for the rest of my life just because I'm blind!"

"I don't expect you to, but you have to get used to being bli – well, you have to get used to this situation before you can move around safely."

"I can't get used to it if I just stay in bed! Anyway, you just admitted that I have to get used to it! So you've all lied to me! I'm going to stay blind!"

Brigitte took a deep breath. "I didn't say that, Ricki! Please, don't twist my words."

"I'm not twisting anything!" The fourteen-year-old made a hand motion absently and accidentally knocked the lamp off the desk onto the floor.

"Watch out!"

Ricki made a face as she heard those words, and Brigitte realized immediately what she had just said.

"I'm sorry. Wait, I ..."

"I can pick it up myself."

Ricki bent down quickly and bumped her forehead against the edge of the desk. "Darn it," she sobbed, and Brigitte, who had taken a step toward her to offer help, forced herself to stand still. Ricki needed to deal with this situation on her own.

"Are you sure I can't help you?" she asked. Ricki exploded.

"NO! Just leave me alone! Please!"

For a few seconds there was silence broken only by the sound of Ricki's heavy breathing.

"You really should be back in bed," Brigitte said after a while. "Not because you can't see, but so that you can get over your virus! Anyway, you're still wobbly-kneed. Fever can make you weak, so it would be good for you to get some rest before we drive to the clinic."

Ricki, who had had a spiteful comment on the tip of her tongue, finally accepted her fate.

"I get it, Mom. Rest and recuperation, with the added benefit that if I stay in bed at least I won't break anything."

"Ricki, please!"

"Well, it's the truth!" Carefully she started to move, hoping to find her bed.

"A little more to the right," Brigitte said softly as Ricki approached the bureau.

*

Josh was frustrated. Of course, Lillian wasn't at home. She was out riding with Holli, as she did every day; at least that's what her mother supposed.

At first he thought about riding over to the Sulais' stable, but then he decided that that didn't make any sense. If she really was out riding with her other friends there was no telling when they would be back.

So Josh just rode around aimlessly. He didn't want to go back home just yet, nor did he want to go back to the Western ranch again. The last thing he wanted was to run into Rebecca again today.

Finally, he decided to go to the movies. At least that would distract him a little.

*

Brigitte had finally reached her husband on the phone, and Marcus had driven home immediately.

Now he was leaving Ricki's room, completely devastated, having tried in vain to cheer up his daughter.

"Why do I feel so ridiculous trying to have a conversation with her? I mean, she's still the same person, but still, I feel so awkward when I'm around her. That's not normal, is it?" Shaking his head, Marcus collapsed onto one of the kitchen chairs and rubbed his hand across his eyes. He wondered if the others had felt the same way when they entered the room for the first time and saw Ricki in her pitiful condition.

Harry, whom Brigitte had told as cautiously as possible that his sister couldn't see, was the only one who actually said what he was really thinking.

"I can't go in there!"

"Why not?" Brigitte asked. "Ricki is still your sister."

"Yeah! But she's different now." Harry looked at his mother from top to bottom. "You guys are all different now, too, after being in her room."

Brigitte took her son in her arms and held him tightly. "That's just because we're worried about her," she tried to explain.

"That's not what it is."

"What is it then?"

"I don't know, but I can feel it."

This answer made Ricki's parents think. They, too, had sensed that something had changed within them, but they were unable to say what it was. The fact that Harry just said it out loud made them afraid.

Of course, Harry felt sorry for his sister because she couldn't see anymore, but also, very quickly, he developed a terrible anger toward her. Why did she have to go blind right now, when he had finally managed to get an A in math? His mom had hardly even noticed.

Chapter 7

Ricki, her nerves stretched to the breaking point, sat stone-faced in the ophthalmologist's consultation room, her hands clasped tightly in her lap, listening carefully to the results of the preliminary examination Dr. Jameson had just performed on her eyes.

Brigitte, with stoic self-control, sat silently and protectively at her side, her arm around her daughter's shoulder. There were a thousand questions buzzing around in her head, but she would wait and listen to what the specialist had to say first. It wasn't easy.

Dr. Jameson explained that further tests would be necessary to determine with absolute certainty what was causing Ricki's loss of vision. But she was going to have to be patient. She hadn't healed sufficiently from the accident to permit the tests to be done just yet.

"Young lady," Dr. Jameson said confidently, "I'll have another look at your pretty eyes in about ten days. We have to wait that long to let the swelling go down completely. If, as I suspect, it is just a matter of eye trauma brought on by various problems occurring all at once, a perfect storm as it were, this will resolve itself. In the meantime, the best you can do is not worry about it."

"And then I'll be able to see again?" Ricki asked, a note of hope in her voice.

The doctor hesitated before answering her. "If the blindness is caused by trauma, yes."

"And if not?"

"Let's not get ahead of ourselves. Let's wait for the results of the next examination, okay?"

Terrific! Ricki thought, as the feeling of hope she'd experienced only a moment before turned into despair and suspicion. It was clear to her that the doctor wasn't being completely truthful with her, that with this talk of "further testing" he was just postponing the inevitable diagnosis: permanent blindness. And no one would be able to change that. She knew it! Her intuition hadn't been wrong! "I ... I feel sick, Mom. Can we go home?"

Brigitte exchanged a look of wordless understanding with the doctor before guiding her daughter gently out of his office. Dr. Jameson's words hadn't raised much hope in her either.

*

In about a week's time, when she'd recovered completely from her bout with the flu and her strength had begun to return, Ricki was beginning to feel okay – physically. She made a conscious effort to go about her daily routine as best she could, given her disability. She learned how to move about within the four walls of her room without breaking anything or injuring herself. When she needed help, she asked for and accepted it gracefully. She didn't complain or go into fits of self-pity, at least not in the presence of others. So it seemed to those around her, her friends and family, that she had come to terms with her blindness.

But it was all just an act to keep her friends from taking pity on her. Deep inside she felt differently. She was beginning to lose any hope of ever returning to the sighted life she'd once known. In her mind's eye, she often called up pictures from the past, saw the colors of the silks at the horse shows, a field of oats in the wind, a sunset, Diablo galloping across the paddock to play with Rashid. But with each passing day these visual memories became less vivid, more difficult to retrieve, and her sense of isolation and depression deepened.

*

Cathy, Lillian, and Kevin came to see Ricki every day, and with each visit they became more comfortable, and less self-conscious in their friend's company. Today, as always, they sat on the floor in Ricki's room, and Kevin regaled his girlfriend with the latest stories about the goings-on at school, while Ricki's unseeing stare, guided by the sound of his voice, fixed on him.

Kevin tried to sound as matter-of-fact as possible, but he kept turning his face away to avoid her blank stare.

"Why do you keep looking away when you talk to me?" Ricki asked sharply, startling Kevin. Lillian and Cathy had surprised looks on their faces, too.

"How did you know that?" Kevin asked. "Can you ... can you see?"

"No, but I'm blind, not deaf!" she snapped. "I can tell from the sound and pitch of your voice whether or not you're looking at me when you talk to me."

"But it's not true. I'm not ..."

"Why are you lying to me?" she asked in a soft, sad voice. "Can't you stand to look at me anymore?"

Kevin turned to Lillian and Cathy. He felt so helpless, so clumsy in his attempts to cheer up his girlfriend. What could he say? He was sure that every word out of his mouth would only make things worse.

He couldn't say, *Ricki, of course I can look at you. Nothing's changed between us.* That wouldn't be quite true. Of course he still adored his girlfriend, but something had changed between them. He was filled with self-doubt. He could no longer be sure whether he was there out of devotion, or pity.

And he was becoming unsure of Ricki's feelings for him as well. Just yesterday, she'd told him she would understand if he wanted to look for a healthy girlfriend, one who could see, be more of a companion to him than she was able to be, someone he could ride and have adventures with. That had hurt him a lot, because it told him Ricki was losing hope that she would ever become an active teenager again.

After a brief, uncomfortable silence, Ricki said, "Mom's made a new appointment at the eye clinic for me. I have to be there in three days."

Kevin breathed a sigh of relief at the change of topic,

although he was surprised that she had mentioned her condition. In the last few days, she had done everything to avoid talking about her blindness.

"Great!" responded Lillian. "I bet you'll be glad when they finally do a thorough examination. I'm sure they'll ..."

"I'm sure they'll say that I could have spared myself the ordeal of the new tests, because they won't do any good!" Ricki finished her girlfriend's sentence.

"Ricki," Cathy offered gently, "maybe it would help if you could see things a little more positively."

"See? Yeah, that *would* be good! Is my glass around here somewhere?" Ricki felt her way to the table.

"One step forward, and then you'll be able to reach it," Lillian answered. She was becoming accustomed to directing her friend in even the smallest of tasks.

"Thanks."

"By the way," Cathy said, trying to change the subject and the mood of the conversation, "I read something interesting yesterday in the new issue of *Young Rider* magazine."

"What was it about?" Kevin asked enthusiastically, glad for the chance to move away from the topic of Ricki's upcoming eye exam.

"Well, it was a profile, really very inspiring, of a young woman, twenty-five-years old, blind since birth, who participates in a full slate of riding activities. She even competes in shows. And she wins ... a lot!"

Lillian and Kevin, astonished at what their friend had just said, stared in disbelief at one another, sharing the same unspoken thought. *What was Cathy thinking! How could she be so thoughtless as to raise this sensitive subject in front of Ricki now?*

"What did you say?" Ricki turned around slowly. "She rides? A blind woman rides in shows?"

Cathy nodded, completely forgetting that her friend couldn't see her.

"A dream," Ricki whispered. For the first time since her accident she could imagine herself in the saddle on Diablo. "Do you ... do you guys think I could do that, too? Well, maybe not participate in a show, but just ... ride?"

Oh, great! Here we go! Cathy, you are a real idiot! Exasperated, Kevin gazed upward at the ceiling.

But Lillian thought she noticed something familiar in Ricki's voice, the tone of enthusiasm and excitement that made her such fun to be around. She sounded more hopeful than she had in a long time. Maybe it hadn't been so thoughtless of Cathy to bring up the subject after all.

"Why not?" Lillian said. "You know you can do anything you set your mind to. And there it is in black and white. It can be done; this woman has told you it can. And what she's saying to you is that if she can do it, so can you."

Kevin couldn't believe it. Now even Lillian was filling Ricki's head with false hope. *This is cruel*, he thought, but to his surprise Ricki's face lit up and her voice became animated, determined.

"Thank you for that, Lillian. You're right! I've been moping around, hiding out in my room, feeling sorry myself. And thanks for sharing that story with me, Cathy. It was

108

just what I needed to pull me out of my self-pity. And it's filled me with a sudden urge to visit Diablo. Maybe I can't see him just now, but that doesn't mean I can't be near him, touch him, feed and groom him." Her longing to be close to Diablo, which she had tried with such effort to suppress, came pouring out of her. "Will you all help me get ready and give me a hand getting to the stable?"

"That's more like it," Lillian said, a clear tone of relief in her voice. "Now you're acting like the Ricki we all know and love. Of course we'll help you. What do you want us to do?"

"Have you seen my stable clothes lying around here anywhere?"

Cathy jumped up and looked around. "I don't see them."

"Darn! Then they're probably in the laundry. It doesn't matter. I'll just go as I am, but let's go, now!"

"Okay!" Cathy took the arm Ricki offered and began to guide her out of the bedroom.

"Kevin? Are you still here? You haven't said anything for a while." Ricki stood still, waiting.

"Where else would I be?" the boy responded.

"What's going on with you, Kevin? You seem so ... distant."

"Oh, nothing, really, it's just ..."

"Just what?"

"Well, I'm just not sure it's a good idea for you to go to the stable right now."

"Kevin, I swear, sometimes you sound just like my mother. What could possibly be wrong with me seeing my horse ... ahh ... visiting him?" she corrected herself.

Kevin didn't have an answer for that, so silently he opened the door and let the girls go out first.

"Let's hope we don't run into Mom," Ricki whispered to her friends. "She'd have a fit if she knew I was going over to visit Diablo!"

The kids crept down the stairs without making any noise, put on their boots, zipped up their warm jackets, and tiptoed out of the house.

*

Jake was fixing the lock on the gate of Rashid's stall when the kids came in.

"Hey, Jake! Look who we've brought with us!" Cathy called out.

The old horseman turned around to see Ricki in the company of her three friends. *They're a foursome again*, he said to himself. *Thank goodness!*

"Girl, I've been praying that you would find your way back here," he said quietly and gave her an awkward hug.

Ricki grinned. "Looks like your prayers were answered. Where's Diablo? Whose stall am I standing in front of right now?"

"Rashid's."

"Oh, then I have to move to the left a little. Wait, let me see if I can do it myself." Ricki groped her way along the boards until she felt Diablo's warm breath on her face and his soft muzzle on her cheek. Tears of joy welled up in her eyes.

"Diablo," she whispered, "I've missed you so much. If only I could see you." She fumbled with the lock on the

110

stall door, opened it, and slipped inside to her horse. *That wasn't too difficult,* she thought to herself, encouraged.

Diablo, sensing that something wasn't quite right with his owner, stood very still as Ricki wrapped her arms around his muscular neck and buried her face in his long mane. "My good boy, the days without you were just awful. You have no idea."

Suddenly, and with determination, Lillian said, "Lead him outside."

"Do what?"

"Lead him outside and tie him up in the corridor. The rope is hanging where it always is."

"And then?" Now Ricki was beginning to get a little panicky. She would have to feel her way out of the stall with her horse, turn him around in the corridor, and then try to find the rope.

"Come on, let's go! You can do it! You just have to go straight ahead, three steps out of the stall, then a turn of about a hundred and sixty degrees, and then four steps diagonally left forward. Then you'll be standing right in front of the rope."

Ricki hesitated. "Am I ready for this?" she wondered aloud.

"Well, if you want to ride, you're going to have to be able to lead your horse by a rope," Lillian added matter-of-factly.

Ricki slid her hand along Diablo's neck until she came to his halter. She grabbed it and said, "Get out of the way, everybody. Here we come!" Then she felt for the door to the stall and slowly led Diablo out into the corridor.

With the help of her memory, and Lillian's instructions, it wasn't difficult for her to find her way to the rope and click it onto the halter with the snap hook.

"Well, guys? How'd I do?" she asked proudly.

Cathy ran to her and gave her a big hug. "Great! Really!"

Ricki beamed. "And now? What should I do next? Should I lead him back in?"

"No!" Lillian wanted Ricki to keep challenging herself. "Go under Diablo's neck and walk ten steps straight ahead into the tack room. Diablo's grooming equipment is just inside the door on the right, where you always keep it. Go get it!"

"Anything for you," Ricki laughed, but then she turned serious and concentrated on her task.

"Keep a little more to the right ... yeah, exactly ... and now straight ahead again ... good! You're almost to the door. About two more steps."

Ricki stretched her hands out in front of her and felt for the doorway. Then she stepped hesitantly inside the tack room. After only a few seconds, she waved her grooming box triumphantly.

"I've got it! Now what?"

"Now come back," Lillian said.

Kevin, who had been skeptical at first, stood beside Jake, wringing his hands nervously as he watched Ricki go slowly and deliberately about the simple tasks Lillian was giving her. *She's got guts! I'll give her that,* he had to admit to himself.

"Okay. I'll do my best," Ricki answered, and she worked her way back into the stable until she could feel Diablo.

"Am I back?"

"What do you think?"

"I think, yes!" Ricki said as she stretched out her hand to stroke Diablo's coat.

"Okay! You can do it!" The sixteen-year old breathed a sigh of relief. "Now all you have to do is groom him!"

A look of dismay came over Ricki's face. "Groom him? How am I supposed to groom a horse when I can't even see where he's dirty?"

Jake interrupted this exchange with loving sternness. "Hey, kids, do I have to remind you of Jake's cardinal rule for the proper care of horses? Always clean and groom your horse *completely*, from front to back and from top to bottom. That way you won't miss any spots, and you'll be able to feel where the coat is matted."

"All right, then, here we go!" she said, and began to comb her horse.

After the mane and the tail had been cleaned with the soft brush, Ricki stepped back and asked, "Is he clean?" When she heard Jake's genuine, "Yes, best grooming job you've ever done," a thrill of excitement went through her. There was stuff she could do, stuff she loved doing and did well; there were possibilities.

"I really did it," she said, leaning against Diablo, exhausted.

"But you forgot something," Lillian scolded. "He also has hooves."

For Kevin, who was beginning to admire Lillian's tough-love approach to Ricki's predicament, this was too much.

"I'll take over cleaning Diablo's hooves," he insisted, but as he reached for the hoof pick he heard Ricki say, "No, you won't."

"What?" he asked, a little perplexed.

"I want to do it myself! You can clean up after me, if you want. I probably won't get everything out." Ricki's voice told him she was in no mood for an argument.

"Be reasonable, Ricki, it could be dangerous. We all know how gentle Diablo is with you, but there's always the chance of a misplaced kick. You've done a lot today. Why risk it? Let me do it."

"No!"

"Jake, come on, help me out here. Say something!" Kevin pleaded, but Jake just shrugged his shoulders.

"If she's determined to try, let her. We're all here to help if she needs us, but my money's on Diablo. He never has, and never will, hurt Ricki, despite what her mother thinks."

"Yeah, I know, but still ..."

"Give me the hoof pick. Please!" Ricki said sharply, and held out her hand.

Kevin still hesitated, but he sensed that Ricki wasn't going to give in.

"Don't you have faith in me, Kevin?" she blurted out.

"Of course I have faith in you! What kind of a question is that?"

"Then prove it and give me that hoof pick!"

Silently, Kevin handed her the tool, but he took a firm grip on Diablo's halter to make sure he didn't move.

"Give it your best shot, Ricki," he said softly.

"Thanks." She slid her hand down her horse's leg, and Diablo, sensing what his owner wanted, obligingly lifted his hoof.

"Picking out the hooves is a real pain when you can't see anything," Ricki said when she'd finished. "You have to feel all around for all the little stones and stuff that get caught under the shoe. Yuck! My hands smell like manure!"

"But you really did a great job," Kevin had to admit.

"And you deserve a reward," Lillian declared. With a knowing wink at Kevin, she gently urged Ricki closer to Diablo.

"What now?" Ricki asked, unaware that Kevin and Lillian were cooking up something.

After a slight hesitation, Kevin stepped over to her, placed her hands on Diablo's broad back, and lifted her left leg.

"Okay, here we go. On three, you're up. Okay?"

Ricki held her breath.

"One ...two ... three ... hop!" Kevin gave Ricki a slight boost onto Diablo's back, and kept his arms firmly around her as she found her seat.

"You do have some faith in me, after all," Ricki whispered, in tears, as she felt her horse beneath her. She bent forward and wrapped her arms around Diablo's neck. "You can't know how happy I am," she cooed into his ear.

Lillian, beaming like a Cheshire cat, gave two thumbs-up – way up. She couldn't remember having had a better day in recent memory.

In her excitement, Cathy slapped Jake on the back, causing him to feign a grimace of pain.

"Sorry, Jake, but I couldn't help myself."

The old man waved her apology aside. "As long as you don't make a habit of it, I can live with it," he said, winking.

Kevin, still standing beside Diablo, was looking up at Ricki in disbelief. He'd never imagined he would see her on horseback again! And now, here she was sitting on her beloved black horse and beaming through her tears of joy.

*

"Ricki? Ricki! Where are you, for heaven's sakes?" they heard someone call.

"Oh no! It's Mom! Hurry, Kevin, help me down," Ricki said and slid down into the arms of her boyfriend.

Lillian had already unsnapped Diablo's halter and led him back to his stall.

"Come on, everybody! Back to the house! And not a word to my mother! Promise?" Ricki was frantic.

"We'll be as silent as the grave. You, too, Jake." Cathy looked at the old man.

"What? Did something happen? I've just been doing my chores, mucking out the stalls, minding my own business. I didn't see anything. Were you here?" he asked innocently, and Lillian grinned.

"That depends on whether Ricki's mother sees us leaving the stable or not. If not, we were at your house visiting you, okay?"

"Okay!" Jake shuffled to the door and looked around the corner. "I don't see anyone. Brigitte must be looking for you inside the house."

"Then let's go. Thanks for everything, Jake. I'll be back soon," Ricki promised. Then she extended her arm, Kevin grabbed it, and the four friends hurried back to the house.

When she opened the front door, Brigitte, panic-stricken at not finding her daughter, breathed a sigh of relief. "Thank goodness. Where have you been? You can't just disappear on me like that!"

Ricki took off her cap. "I just had to go out and get a little fresh air. After all, I've been shut up in my room for over a week. And then we visited Jake. He was really pleased to see me back among the living," Ricki said lightly.

Brigitte was stunned. Why was her daughter in such a good mood all of a sudden?

"Is everything okay, Ricki? You seem so ... so wound up," Brigitte declared, a little puzzled.

"Oh, Mom, I'm fine. It was just nice to be outside, finally. We went for a walk. You know, that works pretty well if I take Kevin's arm," Ricki lied, and squeezed Kevin's arm a little tighter to make her point.

Kevin was uncomfortable with the deception. Brigitte would tear her daughter's head off and her friends' as well if she ever found out what they had been doing in the stable.

I just hope Jake doesn't tell, the boy thought, accompanying Ricki to her room. Then he said good-bye to Lillian and Cathy and left the house, careful to avoid any contact with Brigitte. A lot had happened today. He wanted to be alone to sort things out.

*

He pulled his bike from the bicycle rack at the side of the house, turned on the handlebar headlight, and started to pedal slowly home, the image of Ricki's beaming face strong in his mind's eye. He remembered how touched and impressed he'd been with her courage and determination.

The self-doubt that had plagued him disappeared. *I really do admire her,* he realized. *I don't feel pity ... that's not it. There's nothing pitiful about her, not after the way she performed today.* He knew then that he wanted to be with her always, whether she was sighted or blind. He couldn't wait to see Ricki the next day, give her a hug, and tell her, truthfully, "Of course I'm still crazy about you. Nothing's changed between us."

Chapter 8

Josh was frantic. He'd been trying to reach Lillian by phone for days, but either she wasn't home, had turned off her cell phone, or she just wasn't returning his calls.

For her part, each time she saw his number displayed on her caller ID, Lillian said to herself, *I don't need this. Let him bother Rebecca with his phone calls!*

However, today Josh got lucky.

Lillian was just on her way to the stable when the phone rang and her mother picked up.

"Bates residence. Oh, hello, Josh ... Yes, she's here. Just a moment. Lillian, it's for you," she said, a twinkle in her eye.

Oh, Mom, if you only knew, thought Lillian. She let a couple of beats go by before she took the phone from her mother's hand.

"What's up?" she said curtly.

"Lillian, where have you been? I've been trying to reach you every day! I'd almost given up hope of you ever answering the phone."

"I didn't. Mom did. But now that you've got me, what do you want?" she said, making no effort to conceal her irritation.

Josh was puzzled by Lillian's coldness. Had someone told her about his crush on Rebecca? "I just wanted to ask when we're going to see each other."

"Why would we want to do that?"

"Excuse me! Is there something wrong with wanting to see your girlfriend, at least once in a while?" Josh asked, glad they were having this conversation over the phone and not face to face. At least she couldn't see that he was beginning to sweat, that he was embarrassed, and that his face had turned beet red.

"Girlfriend?" Lillian asked, drawing out the word. When Josh didn't answer, she said, "If it's a girlfriend you're looking for, then maybe you should call Rebecca. I'm sure you have her number."

Oh no, she knows! "Lillian, I don't know what you think or what you've been told ..." he began, but the girl cut him dead.

"Since you say you don't know what I think, let me tell you." Her pent-up hurt, anger, and resentment were beginning to find their voice. "You've been mooning over her since she showed up. Everybody's noticed it. You talk about her all, I mean, *all* the time. You compare me to her unfavorably as a rider because she rides Western style – big deal – and I don't. And then I see the two of you in each other's arms in front of Ringo's stall, and you want me to believe I'm still your girlfriend?" She'd worked herself into a full-throated fury. "You lie to me and then you expect me to be overjoyed because you think it might be nice for us to get together? Well, forget it!" And with that, she hung up.

"Lillian, please, we've got to talk!" Josh yelled into a dead phone.

Well, that's that, thought Lillian, but the satisfaction she expected to feel from telling Josh off didn't come, because, given what she'd said to him – and the way she'd said it – it seemed unlikely she'd ever see him again. And despite everything that had happened, that was an unbearable prospect.

"Are you alright?" her mother asked, dumbfounded. She'd never heard her daughter yell at anyone with such vehemence before.

"Yeah, yeah, Mom, everything's just great," Lillian said tonelessly. Then she hurried off to the stable before her mother could start asking her a thousand questions.

*

"Harry's at a friend's house and Mom is getting her hair done. This is the best possible time to go to the stable without getting caught," Ricki said to Kevin, as he lay sprawled on the floor of her room.

He'd made a point of getting to Ricki's way ahead of the others. He needed time alone with her, to tell her – finally, openly, and honestly – about the jumble of emotions he'd been going through since her accident.

"Remember the other day when you asked me what was going on with me ... that I'd become so distant? That was a fair question, and I blew it because I didn't know myself. But when I saw you and Diablo together ..."

121

Ricki fumbled to find his face, took it gently in both hands, stared sightlessly at him, and said softly, "Stop, Kevin. There's no need. I know you all love me. You and Cathy and Lillian proved that to me yesterday in the stable. I don't feel like an outsider anymore; in fact I feel closer to you all than I ever have..."

This quiet moment was shattered by the sudden appearance of Cathy and Lillian, who burst into the room. "Would you just look at those two," Cathy blurted. "Well, I never ..." she said with mock disapproval.

"Hi, Cathy. Is Lillian with you?" asked Ricki.

"Yeah, I'm here, too," Lillian answered listlessly.

Ricki listened closely. Since she'd lost her sight, she'd become much more aware of the telltale inflections in people's voices. The doctor had told her that might happen. "What's wrong, Lily? You sound so down."

"Nothing's wrong."

Ricki was unconvinced. "Come on, tell us," she urged.

"If you must know, I just broke up with Josh," Lillian blurted out.

Ricki was silent for a moment, and then she said quietly, "But you still care for him. I can hear it in your voice."

Lillian's face turned bright red. "It doesn't matter what you think you hear," she answered a little too forcefully. "I don't like him anymore – at all!"

"Yes, you do. You wouldn't be this upset if you didn't."

"Think whatever you like!"

"Well, I will," Ricki continued, "and what I think is you should try to swallow your hurt and your pride and talk to him and let him talk to you. There's no question that he behaved badly, but you know how easily some guys can become ... shall we say, distracted. I'm sure that's all Rebecca is to Josh. And Josh is too great a guy to lose to a distraction. Talk to him. Face to face."

"No way," wailed Lillian. "How can I? He'd probably hang up on me if I called him now, after what I said to him." She was in tears.

"You don't know that. I'm sure he's in a pretty bad place right now, too. You never can tell. There's a good chance he'd be relieved to hear from you. My advice is for you to take the chance," Ricki urged forcefully.

Ricki makes a lot of sense; she always does, Lillian mused to herself. *I may be the oldest member of this crew, but, hands down, Ricki is the wisest.*

"I'll consider it. Now," she said, changing the subject abruptly, "do you feel like going to the stable today, Ricki?"

"Yes. Right away, before my mother gets back from town."

"Okay, what are we waiting for?"

Kevin got up, took Ricki by the arm, and hurried after Lillian and Cathy, who were already on their way downstairs.

"Hey, Cathy, we haven't heard anything about Hal lately," Ricki remarked on her way to the stalls. "Are you two dating? And have you seen him recently?"

Cathy's eyes began to shine. "He calls me every day. At the moment, he can't come to Mercy Ranch. He has an exchange student from France staying at his house. But he said that the guy will be gone in a week, and then he'll have all the time in the world for me. I can't wait to see him again!"

"It doesn't look as though Jake is here," Kevin noted as he and Ricki stood directly in front of Diablo's stall, "but Diablo is ready and waiting for you."

"Hey, my boy. Everything okay with you? Happy to see me?"

"What a silly question," laughed Cathy. "Of course, he is. At least as happy as you are to be with him!"

"He can hardly wait for you to brush him again," Lillian added.

"Thanks, that's what I wanted to hear," Ricki said, grinning, and then she felt for the bolt on the gate in order to open it.

Lillian navigated her and Diablo out onto the corridor, then to the tack room and back. While Ricki worked on Diablo's coat, the others groomed their horses as well. To Kevin, it seemed almost like the old days, when the four of them would ready their horses for some cross-country riding, back when Ricki could still see.

"I want to saddle him," Ricki said abruptly.

"What?" Kevin stared at her. "Right now?"

"Yes, of course right now."

"So why don't you just do it?" she heard coming from Holli's stall.

Ricki hesitated. Lillian seemed to have anticipated that Ricki would want to do this.

"Okay," Ricki replied slowly. "Why don't I just do it?" Without waiting for someone to direct her, she began walking toward the tack room, counting her steps.

Made it! she cheered silently as she entered the tack

room and let her hands glide over the saddles. She stood still at the third one. She felt for the sheepskin that she'd fitted around the girth and was delighted that she was able to locate Diablo's saddle so quickly. His snaffle was right beneath it, and she hung it over her shoulder before she laid the saddle over her arm.

"This thing is pretty heavy when you carry it on one arm," she said to herself, and felt her way out of the room and back to the corridor, where her friends looked at her silently. They were anxious to see how far Ricki would get on her own.

Kevin stood by, waiting to help if Ricki needed him, but he knew how important it was for her to gain a sense of independence. So he kept a close watch on her, but he also kept his distance.

"Oh, darn!" Ricki said, stumbling over her grooming box, which she had forgotten to put away. She almost fell down. But at the last moment she caught herself. She pushed the box close to the stall wall, and then she ducked under Diablo's neck and stood on his left side.

"Now what?" she asked a little awkwardly.

"Now do what you said you wanted to do," Lillian said emphatically. "Saddle your horse."

"Yeah, but how?"

"How do you think? Like you always do. Just try it."

"Okay." Ricki took a deep breath, and then she walked over to Diablo's shoulder and felt over his withers with her hand. Then she lifted the saddle onto his back carefully and moved it back and forth until she was satisfied that the fit was correct. Next she pulled the girth down under the horse's belly and buckled it loosely.

It seemed to her that it was taking an eternity, but finally she had managed it. Exhausted, she leaned against Diablo's neck for a moment. Ricki felt the headpiece still hanging over her shoulder.

"And I'll get that on, too," she said, determined, even though at the moment she wasn't convinced that she could. She slid her hand over Diablo's head, opened the clasp on the side of the halter, and pulled it over the horse's ears. She put on Diablo's snaffle, making sure that all the straps were in the right places. When she had finally pulled the reins over his neck, her friends applauded her.

"Wow, Ricki, that was great! You really did it!"

"Congratulations!" Kevin couldn't stop himself. Quickly, he walked over to his girlfriend and gave her a quick hug. "That was an amazing performance," he said.

Ricki smiled happily. "And what is the reward today?"

Kevin hesitated for a moment. Then he took off Diablo's halter, grabbed the reins, and took Ricki's hand.

"For this magnificent performance, there is a special prize," he said grandly, and he winked at Cathy and Lillian, who had already guessed what was coming next.

"What?" Ricki asked excitedly.

"Come with me and I'll show you," Kevin commanded.

Ricki's heart beat faster as she left the stable with Kevin and Diablo.

"Now, mount your horse," the boy challenged her, as he held down the stirrup.

"Are you serious?"

"Of course I'm serious. Come on, let's go!"

Ricki felt for the left stirrup and then shakily she put her foot inside. Then she pulled herself up into the saddle and grabbed the ends of the reins.

"Maybe you should start by holding onto his mane," Kevin suggested. "Are you comfortable?" he asked. When Ricki nodded yes, he circled the paddock twice, with Diablo on a rope, before he led the other two out of the paddock and onto open ground. He planned to lead Ricki on a wonderful ride with her horse in the crisp winter air.

"Just look at them! Isn't that fabulous?" Cathy asked dreamily, watching the three of them from the stable doorway.

"Yes," Lillian agreed. "Finally, Ricki looks like she's where she belongs."

*

Ricki sat silently on Diablo, enjoying the swaying motion of the horse and the warm rays of the sun that caressed her face, and she closed her eyes.

"I wish this ride would never end," she said very softly. "I never appreciated before how precious everything is. I took it all for granted, but right now I am so grateful for this moment."

Kevin's hand squeezed Diablo's reins. What wouldn't he give if only Ricki could see again?

"Where are we?" the girl asked.

"Behind the paddock, opposite the Bates's orchard."

"What? We've gone that far already? Isn't this too much for you? I mean, after all, you have to walk the whole way back, too." Ricki was beginning to feel guilty about putting Kevin through all this.

"It's okay." Kevin kept plodding through the snow.

With a start, the girl remembered her mother.

"I think we should turn around and head back," she said. "We don't want my mother to get home before us. She would be furious!"

Kevin stopped short. "I completely forgot about her! Okay, let's go back. But don't think this is the last time we'll go for a ride like this." Immediately, he turned the horse around in a wide arc.

"Oh, that sounds great!" Ricki was already looking forward to the next time. "Maybe you could ride Sharazan and take Diablo on a lead rope, after I've gotten into the saddle. I'm beginning to feel pretty sure of myself."

"We'll definitely do that. But for now, I feel safer walking next to Diablo."

"Okay. But let's not forget about it, okay? I would so love to go riding with you guys again!"

"Don't worry, I won't forget. We all – Cathy, Lillian, and I – want that too."

*

"It was just dreamy!" raved Ricki, two hours later, as the friends were sitting in her room together. "Thank you so much, Kevin! And you two as well, of course," she said, turning toward Lillian and Cathy. "For everything! Without you guys, I'd probably still be sitting here feeling sorry for myself and trying to cope with my fate!"

"Oh, come on, get off it, what 'fate'? Who believes

in that nonsense?" Cathy said. "Starting the day after tomorrow, you're going to feel like you've been reborn!"

"The day after tomorrow? How come?"

"Well, after you've been to the eye clinic, and they tell you that you're going to see again."

Kevin held his breath. Cathy was on thin ice making that assertion. None of the doctors who had examined her had gone so far as to guarantee that she'd see again.

"Oh, that's what you meant," Ricki said, too happy at the moment to start thinking about the eye clinic. "I had completely forgotten about that."

"You forgot?" Lillian's voice sounded incredulous. "How can you forget something like that? I mean, this is a matter of –"

"I know what's at stake, Lillian," Ricki said, turning serious. "I'm not an idiot, but honestly, I just don't want to think about it right now. I don't want to get my hopes up only to have them shattered. I'd rather try to deal with my situation as it exists right now, and not think about 'What if –?'"

"Maybe you're right to think that way," responded Cathy after a pause.

"Look, I was so happy riding a little while ago, that if I begin to focus on the situation with my eyes I'll lose that wonderful feeling I had sitting on Diablo. It's beginning to fade already anyway. What a shame."

Lillian and Cathy looked at each other. They felt awful.

"I'm so sorry, Ricki," said Lillian softly. "We have to learn to deal with this situation, too. We're sorry for talking about it again."

"That's okay," answered the girl and leaned against Kevin. "It won't be the last time I have to deal with the topic, even though I don't like to think about it."

*

"Did you do anything fun while I was gone?" Brigitte asked Ricki in the evening, as the family sat at the dinner table with Jake.

"Well, Lillian, Cathy, and Kevin came by, as usual. We ... we went for a little walk."

Noticing that Ricki was having trouble finding the platter of pot roast on the table, Brigitte asked, "Would you like me to fix you a plate?"

"No thanks, Mom. I'm fine," Ricki answered.

"I called the blacksmith and asked him to come by," Jake said, trying to make conversation.

That got Ricki's attention. "When's he coming?"

"Sometime next week. Probably Thursday, but he'll let me know."

Brigitte looked disapprovingly at Jake. She didn't want the subject of horses brought up around Ricki.

"Would you like something to drink, Ricki?" Marcus was holding the pitcher of lemonade in his hand, but his daughter declined.

Harry, who was still having problems dealing with his sister's blindness, kept his eyes glued to his plate, but now, feeling neglected, he exploded.

"How come no one asks me what I'd like to drink or if they should make up a plate for me? And isn't anyone interested in what *I* did this afternoon?" Then he looked directly at his sister. "Why don't you tell Mom the truth? That you were in the stable and groomed Diablo."

Brigitte turned pale. "You did *what*?"

How did Harry know that she had been in the stable? And why was he being so nasty and telling on her, when he knew exactly how his mother would react?

Harry slammed his glass onto the table and ran up to his room.

"You were near the horses? Didn't I tell you that's too dangerous when you can't see anything?" Brigitte's voice was almost a screech.

"Calm down, everybody," Marcus said, assuming his customary role as peacemaker. He was pleased to see that his daughter's depression had lifted and that she seemed to be taking more interest in life around her. "What can it hurt?"

"What can it hurt? Do you have any idea what could have happened?"

Jake cleared his throat and took Ricki's hand under the table. *Here it comes*, he thought. "I was there, too, Brigitte," he said reassuringly. "So were Kevin, Cathy, and Lillian. You should have seen the way the kids helped and looked out for Ricki. We wouldn't have let anything happen to her, and anyway –"

"So," Brigitte cut him off, "you were a part of this conspiracy, too! That's terrific! I should have known. Would you have also accepted the responsibility if Ricki had been trampled?"

"Mom, please, don't get so worked up. We're talking about Diablo. He wouldn't trample anyone, least of all me."

131

"Oh, sure! And your Diablo is a such a lamb, anyway, isn't he!"

"He is!"

"Ricki, stop it! Don't argue with me." Brigitte's anxiety was completely overriding her reason. "For the time being, you will stay out of the stalls! Do you understand me?"

Ricki said nothing. Placing her hands on the table to steady herself, she pushed herself slowly into an upright position. Had she been able to see, she would have walked briskly – and defiantly – to the stable, but the best she could do was stumble toward the kitchen door, or at least in the direction she thought it was.

"Stop!" Marcus called out just as she was about to bump into the wall. "Let me help you upstairs," he said softly and led her out before Brigitte could say anything more.

Jake was becoming increasingly irritated with Brigitte. Couldn't she see that her overprotective rules were getting in the way of Ricki having a normal, active life? He couldn't be silent.

"You really overdo it, Brigitte," Jake said brusquely, as he pushed his chair back from the table and stood up. "Instead of being happy about Ricki's progress, you take the joy out of even her smallest pleasure. And maybe you should pay more attention to your son, and explain to him that blind people need a little more attention, a little more consideration, than those of us who can see."

"Don't you dare tell me what I should or shouldn't do, Jake!"

"You've known me a while, Brigitte," he began in a conciliatory tone. "You treat me – I feel – like a member

132

of the family. I love these kids as if they were my own grandchildren. But when it comes to their welfare, I will speak my mind! Your constant coddling of Ricki is holding her back! Good night!" Upset, he left the kitchen. A moment later they all heard the front door slam shut.

"And once again, I'm the bad guy! Terrific!" Furious, Ricki's mother balled up her napkin and threw it across the table. Then she covered her eyes with both hands and reflected on what had just happened. In her mind's eye she saw Carlotta standing in front of her and shaking her head.

"You still haven't learned anything!" she remembered Carlotta saying to her. *"When are you going to understand that horses sense when there is something wrong and they react with acute sensitivity to danger? Horses aren't a problem. The trauma you experienced when you were young has made them a problem. You should have more trust in Diablo! He would never hurt Ricki!"*

"It's all so easy for the rest you," Brigitte whispered, immediately ashamed of herself for making that remark. It wasn't easy for anybody. She knew that. Her anger was spent and the only thing she felt was remorse over how she had reacted.

She sighed deeply, and then decided to go upstairs and ask her daughter to forgive her. Yes, and then ... then she would go to Harry's room and try to talk with him about what his sister, and the whole family, were dealing with now.

But the thought that Ricki would probably be with her horse again tomorrow filled her with anxiety. *I don't think I can let her out of my sight anymore,* she thought as she climbed the stairs. *I'd never be able to forgive myself if anything more happened to her.*

*

Ricki was glad to be alone in her room – finally.

She'd had a long talk with her parents. Of course, she understood that Brigitte's fears for her safety came out of her love for her. It was clear to Ricki, however, that she was not going to stop taking care of Diablo because of them. Either she would have to visit him secretly in the stable or she would have to find someone who would support her wishes; someone who had some influence on her mother.

"I don't understand why Mom can't see that my working with Diablo is the best therapy for me," she said to herself.

Ricki sat on her bed, leaned against the wall, wrapped her arms around her knees and started to think things over. Maybe if she could prove to her mother just how much Diablo could achieve for her ... The only question was how to do this.

Suddenly her face lit up. "That could work!" Excited, she pulled her cell phone out of her pant's pocket, felt the keypad, and then dialed the stored number, thinking she had called Carlotta. But it turned out to be someone completely different.

"Oh, Josh, I'm sorry. I didn't mean to dial your number. I thought I had dialed Carlotta. This is Ricki, by the way!"

Josh laughed. "It happens. But I'm glad to hear from you. How are you? I haven't talked to you in a while."

Ricki hesitated. Could it be that Lillian hadn't told him she was blind?

134

"Oh, as good as can be expected, I guess," she replied.

"Great! Hey, Ricki, could you do me a really huge favor?"

"And that would be?"

"Lillian ... she's really mad at me!"

"Does she have a reason to be?"

Josh was silent for a moment. "Not really. Well, I mean ... I would like to talk with her and explain some things, but she won't let me near her. Could you tell her that she should at least listen to what I have to say?"

"What about Rebecca?" Ricki wanted to know.

"What about her? There isn't anything to tell ... well, almost nothing."

"'Almost nothing'? What's that supposed to mean? Josh, you have to be straight with me if you want me to help you guys."

Josh could understand that, so he decided to tell Ricki everything.

When he'd finished recounting the story of his crush on Rebecca and Lillian's reaction when he called her, Ricki was impressed with his honesty, and she promised him she'd do all she could so that he and Lillian could at least have a conversation together.

"Do you still care for her? Lillian, I mean."

"Yes!" Josh responded with all his heart.

"She cares for you, too," Ricki said, and she could imagine how Josh felt at that moment. "Okay, I'll do my best."

"Ricki, thank you so much! I owe you. Why don't you pick out a pair of riding gloves in the shop? Maybe a pair of those new neon ones. They come in five different colors."

"Thanks, Josh, that's nice of you, but I don't care about the color."

"How come? I don't think you'd like the poisonous green ones!" he laughed.

"Josh, you could sell me poisonous green-purple ones and I wouldn't even notice."

"How come? Are you blind or something?" he joked. He almost choked when Ricki said, "Yes."

"You're not serious, Ricki! Don't joke about that, okay?"

"It isn't a joke, Josh, but don't worry about it. They're not sure it's a permanent condition."

"Well, that's a relief."

"We'll keep in touch, okay? Now I have to call Carlotta." She didn't feel like talking about her blindness at the moment. She said a hasty good-bye to Josh, who stared at his cell phone in disbelief at what he'd just been told.

Ricki, on the other hand, realized that Josh was the first person she had told that her blindness might not be permanent. Suddenly she felt a certain hope begin to blossom within her. Maybe the doctors at the clinic would be able to help her after all.

That would be wonderful, she thought longingly, but then she remembered what she had started to do. Quickly she touched another button on her phone and this time it was the right number.

"Mercy Ranch, Carlotta Mancini speaking."

"Hi, Carlotta. It's me, Ricki."

"Hello, Ricki. What's up? How are you?"

"Thanks, I'm okay. I groomed and saddled Diablo today,

and then Kevin took us out for a ride. It was so wonderful to ride again, but you can't tell on me! Mom freaked out just hearing that I was in the stable and groomed Diablo!"

"You got him ready to ride all by yourself?" asked Carlotta, fascinated.

"Yes, of course! I didn't think I could do it either."

"That's wonderful. Ricki, that's fantastic! The only thing that bothers me is your mother's reaction. I thought we had sorted that out a few days ago, but apparently I have to have another talk with her."

"Oh, yes, Carlotta, please do. That would really be nice of you. But I need you to do me another favor."

"Of course. What is it?"

"I want to show Mom that she doesn't need to be afraid when I'm around Diablo, and I thought ..."

Chapter 9

Ricki heard a tentative knocking on her bedroom door.

"Yeah?" she answered still half asleep. "What time is it?"

"A little past six." It was Harry.

Ricki shot up in bed. "Harry? What are you doing here at this hour?"

Embarrassed, her brother walked up to the bed. "I have to get dressed and have breakfast before the school bus comes," he stammered, "but I want to apologize to you before I go for what I said yesterday ... and for the whole thing."

Ricki didn't know to say.

"I thought you were doing it on purpose!"

"What did you think I was doing on purpose?" Ricki asked, astonished.

"Well, not being able to see."

"Harry, you don't just decide whether or not you can see."

"I thought you were just pretending so you'd get all the attention from Mommy and Daddy!"

Ricki shook her head. Was Harry really such a baby that he truly believed what he was telling her? That just couldn't be!

"Harry, you don't really think that anyone in her right mind would pretend to be blind and get bruises all over her body just to take advantage of her younger brother, do you?"

"I don't know," Harry said, unsure of himself. "But now that I know you really can't see anything, well ...what's it like not being able to see?" His curiosity had gotten the better of him.

Ricki reached out her hand to her brother, and, after hesitating for a moment, he put his in hers.

"It's horrible," Ricki said quietly. "And when you reach out your hand, you're happy if someone grabs hold of it. At least then you can feel them even if you can't see them."

Harry closed his eyes for a moment and felt the warmth of his sister's hand.

"Now I feel you, too," he said. "Are you still mad at me?"

Ricki attempted a smile. "No, Harry." And suddenly she had an idea. "But you could help me ... to make up for yesterday."

"Of course. Anything." He desperately wanted a chance to make up for his bad behavior.

"I'll let you know this afternoon, okay? You get ready for school now, and I'd like to go back to sleep for a while."

"Okay! 'Bye, Ricki! And thank you!" he called over his shoulder as he ran back to his room.

*

The closer it got to the time for her friends' visit, the

more nervous Ricki became. She stood at the window and listened for the familiar sound of their voices, but everything was quiet.

I hope Carlotta gets here on time, Ricki said, crossing her fingers. If only she knew what time it was now. She was convinced her mother would become suspicious if she kept asking her for the time.

Finally she heard the engine of Carlotta's old Mercedes, and about ten minutes later she came into Ricki's room.

"Hi, Carlotta. Thanks for coming." Ricki hoped that she was smiling in the right direction.

"Hello, dear. Your mother is downstairs making us some coffee, which means that we'll probably sit and talk afterward. I've already chosen a great topic." Carlotta's eyes twinkled, but then she turned serious. "Are you sure the thing you're planning is a good idea? I mean, it could go completely haywire, and then your mother would never let you go into the stable or be around Diablo again."

"Actually, she's pretty much done that already, but I need you to get her to change her mind voluntarily. You're the only one who can convince her how important riding and Diablo are for me."

"Let's hope that's true. Believe me, I'll do my best, but I can't guarantee that it will work. You have to understand that."

Ricki sighed and lowered her head. "If you can't do it, no one can. By the way, don't be surprised if Harry shows up in the kitchen and starts really getting on Mom's nerves! That's part of my plan."

140

Carlotta grinned. "Oh? Are you two getting along again? I'm glad to hear that."

"Yes. This morning he came by and apologized. He can't wait to make up for what he said yesterday."

Carlotta laughed. "That's what I like to hear! Okay, I'll go down to the lioness's den. When do you guys plan on going to the stable?"

"If it were up to me, right away, but the others aren't here yet. Oh, by the way, I'm going to send Cathy to the kitchen to ask Mom for a can of soda. So, when you see her, you'll know it's starting."

"Okay, Ricki dear. I'll keep my fingers crossed that everything goes as planned."

Ricki nodded.

She heard Carlotta's footsteps moving away and then the door closing softly. She hadn't told her that none of her friends knew of the plan yet. She could only hope that they would go along with it. But first, they had to get here!

*

"Are you insane, Ricki?" Cathy asked, shaking her head. "What do you think your mom is going to do when she sees you riding Diablo? This is the craziest plan you've ever had ... and you've had some pretty crazy plans over the past few years."

"But when she sees that I can manage even though I'm blind, maybe she won't be scared anymore."

"Nonsense! When it comes to horses, your mother is always in a panic. You know that. Even when you were completely healthy, she shook with fear every time you went out riding."

"Then it's about time she got over it!" Ricki countered stubbornly.

"Well, I think she'll figure out what's going on beforehand, and then it'll be all over anyway!" added Lillian. "Besides, you're trying to do in one day what the girl in the riding magazine article achieved only after years of training. That's impossible!"

"But Carlotta and Harry are there to keep Mom from noticing anything too early. They're supposed to keep her from showing up every five minutes to ask me if everything's okay. And I don't intend to gallop across the front yard. I've already explained what I want to do. Nothing more and nothing less."

Kevin looked at Ricki with concern, but he knew that she would do what she had planned, no matter what. If her friends didn't help her, she would try it alone, and that would be much more dangerous than the plan she'd concocted.

"Let's try it. In theory, nothing should go wrong," he said slowly. Ricki squeezed his hand gratefully.

"Okay, then let's not waste any more time. Cathy, please go downstairs to the kitchen and ask my Mom for a can of soda. That's the sign for Carlotta that the show's begun."

Lillian looked at Ricki, amazed. "You've thought of everything, haven't you?"

"Of course!" Ricki said, but she couldn't hide her excitement. All her hopes were on Carlotta. Up to now, Carlotta had been the only one who'd ever been able to get Brigitte to change her mind. Maybe ... just maybe, she could work that miracle one more time.

*

The friends slipped out of the house through the patio door rather than leave by way of the kitchen, where Brigitte and Carlotta were engaged in serious conversation. As fast as they could they ran across to the stable.

Jake was astonished to see the girl dressed in her full riding gear.

"Planning something big?" he asked curiously.

"Yes! But you didn't see anything. It would probably be best if you went over to your house so that you don't have to get involved in any of this."

"You'd like that, wouldn't you? No one ever tells me anything," Jake said, disgusted.

"Oh, Jake, don't be like that. I just don't want to get you into trouble with Mom," replied Ricki.

The old horseman helped the girl move to one side as Kevin led Sharazan out into the corridor to groom him and saddle him. Lillian and Cathy did the same with Diablo.

"Aha!" Jake suddenly understood what Ricki was planning to do.

"You're going to ride him? Does your mother know about this?"

Ricki shook her head. "Not yet, but she'll find out soon enough."

"I don't know how you're planning to let her know, especially after last night. Have you already forgotten about that?"

"How could I? But look, if I don't do this, then Mom is going to forbid me ever to ride again, or at least she'll always be afraid for me, even if the doctors at the eye clinic are able to restore my sight. But if I can prove to her that I can trust Diablo blindly," she said with bitter irony, "then maybe –"

"Finished! We can go!" Kevin interrupted Ricki's speech.

"Diablo's saddled, too!" Lillian gave the thumbs up and Cathy stepped aside.

"I just hope you're doing the right thing, child." Jake didn't feel comfortable with Ricki's plan at all.

"Wish us luck!"

While Kevin and Lillian led the horses out into the courtyard, Cathy accompanied Ricki outside. Two minutes later Kevin and his girlfriend were sitting in the saddle.

Jake stood in the doorway of the stable. "I just hope nothing happens," he kept murmuring to himself.

*

In the meantime, Carlotta and Brigitte were already on their second cup of coffee, and they were talking excitedly about the town's upcoming rummage sale. Items were going to be sold at a flea market and the proceeds were going to several local charities.

Brigitte was happy. "You can't imagine how glad I am to finally get rid of all the old stuff that's been filling up the attic!"

"Well, you know what they say," Carlotta offered, "One person's trash is another person's treasure."

"Well, then, we should raise a lot of money, don't you –" For a moment Brigitte hesitated. "It's so quiet in the house. I wonder what the kids are up to? Maybe I should go upstairs and check on them. I don't want Ricki to get the idea of going over to the stable again!"

Oops, thought Carlotta.

"Oh, come on, let them be," she tried to stop Brigitte. "We were young once, too, remember, and we couldn't stand it when our mothers kept coming to the door to check on us. They're probably telling each other who's in love with whom! You'd definitely be in the way."

"But I have such an uneasy feeling. I'll be right back." She was just getting up from her chair when Harry came running in.

"Mommy, can you play a game of chess with me now? You promised me yesterday. You said you would for sure."

Carlotta breathed a sigh of relief. That was close!

"Yes, I know, but at the moment ..."

"You *promised* me! You said this afternoon, when I finished my homework, and I just finished it!"

"Harry, you can see that I have company right now."

"Carlotta isn't company, she's family!"

"Oh, thank you, young man. That makes me feel very good," the former circus rider laughed.

"It's true! Do you mind if Mommy plays a game of chess with me?" Harry looked at her intently.

"Not at all."

"See? Carlotta doesn't mind."

Brigitte rolled her eyes in frustration. "Couldn't you teach Carlotta to play the game?"

"Oh, no! I'm much too old for things like that," Carlotta rejected the suggestion out of hand.

"We'll play tonight, okay?" Brigitte promised again, but Harry wasn't having any of it.

"Great! First you explain to me ... promise me ... that

145

you're going to make more time for me in the future, and then you don't do it!" Harry said in his best hurt little boy voice.

Carlotta nodded to Brigitte. "If you promised him, then play the game with him. It won't take that long, and as long as the coffee lasts I'll be completely satisfied."

"Well, okay. All right, Harry, set it up, but only *one* game, okay?"

Harry beamed. "Okay!" He ran out of the kitchen and then reappeared with the game board and chess set.

"Carlotta, did you know that I plan to become the world chess champion?"

"No, really? That's a very ambitious goal."

"You bet! Mommy doesn't stand a chance against me!"

"Then why do I have to play at all?" asked Brigitte, winking, and got up from her chair.

"Where are you going?" Harry asked suspiciously.

"Excuse me, Mr. World Champion, but I drank too much coffee, and now I have to go to the bathroom so that I don't have to interrupt our game later on."

"Okay, but hurry!"

"Of course!" Brigitte winked at Carlotta and left the kitchen.

"Well, how am I doing?" asked Harry quietly.

Carlotta nodded in admiration at him. "Try to make the game last as long as possible."

"Okay, but I'll have to really work hard at it. Mommy's a terrible chess player."

*

Kevin held Diablo on the lead reins beside Sharazan, so close that his knees almost touched Ricki's knees. The two horses walked next to each other at a moderate pace as the boy made them go in a wide arc around the snow-covered courtyard.

"How do you feel?" he kept asking her.

"Okay. With every step a little better. As long as you don't try any sharp curves, I won't have any problems with my balance," Ricki answered, her nerves taut. She held the reins at the length she felt was right so that Diablo would become accustomed to the bit.

"Let's try a trot," she said all of a sudden. "But a slow one, okay?"

"Good. Are you tight in the saddle?"

"Yes!"

Kevin let his roan trot, and Diablo kept up with him. At first Ricki did a sitting trot, but then she realized that she felt more sure of herself when she posted.

"Are you still okay?"

"Of course!"

They went around about three times at a trot. Then Kevin gave the command to rein in the horses, and changed to a direction that would lead them straight across the yard.

"Yikes, left hand. All of a sudden that's a weird feeling," said Ricki after a while.

"Should we ride the other way around?"

"No, no, it's okay. I have to get used to it... You know what? It's going better than I thought it would. I'd love to try a canter!"

Kevin hesitated. "No, Ricki," he said firmly "First of

all, the ground is too icy, second, you haven't had enough training yet, and third, you know what you promised me – no cantering! No taking risks!"

Ricki sighed. "Yeah, I know. Still, I'd really like to try."

"But not today!"

"Okay, okay! Then let's trot a little more. I think I'll be ready for my mom in about ten minutes."

"You think so?"

"Yeah!"

"Well, okay, then ... uh-oh ... wait a minute, my saddle is sliding. I have to tighten the girth." Kevin said, and he directed both of the horses into the middle of the yard and made them stop.

"Do you think I can let you go for a moment?" asked the boy. When Ricki nodded he pressed the lead reins into her hand, laid his left leg in front of the saddle, and began to tighten the girth.

"Okay, I'm done," he said only a few seconds later, and was just sitting back in the saddle when the house door flew open and a scream cut through the air.

*

"Mommy's taking a long time in the bathroom," Harry declared innocently, and Carlotta started having a bad feeling.

"Maybe I should – " she began, when the scream suddenly interrupted her sentence.

Harry's and Carlotta's glance met in a fraction of a second.

"Oh, no!" Carlotta got up as quickly as she could. Harry threw the chess pieces he had in his hands onto the table and ran outside. Carlotta, leaning on her cane, was a lot slower.

*

Brigitte couldn't hear any of the noises she was accustomed to hearing when Ricki's friends came to visit. *No music ... no laughing. Hmmm, I wonder what's going on*, she thought to herself. Following her instincts, she headed for the stable. When she saw Ricki on Diablo, she screamed in fear.

"RICKI! NO!"

Sharazan, who was still standing on a long rein in the middle of the yard with his head down, was spooked when he heard the sudden scream. He jerked his head up and sprang to the side, even though Diablo stood there and was blocking him. He bumped hard into the black horse, who then tried to escape a collision with his stable mate by rearing up on his hind legs.

Ricki wasn't prepared for this. She lost her seat and fell out of the saddle.

Kevin got Sharazan under control quickly and jumped down from his horse, while Lillian and Cathy and Jake came running over.

"Who screamed?" shouted Cathy.

"Oh, no, Ricki!" shouted Lillian. What had happened to Ricki? Lillian slid to a stop and knelt down beside her girlfriend, who, though a little startled, didn't appear to be hurt.

Brigitte was still standing in the doorway, and looked at what was happening in the courtyard as if she were in a trance.

"What's going on? Did you scream like that, Mommy?" called Harry behind her. He stopped short when he saw Ricki lying on the ground.

149

Carlotta was standing beside Brigitte.

"What happened? Why did you ... heavens! Ricki!" Carlotta turned pale. Her fears were realized.

"She ... she was ... on that horse. I had forbidden her ..." Brigitte stammered in shock at the sight of her daughter lying on the ground at Diablo's feet.

"Come on!" Carlotta took her arm and pulled her along.

"I'm okay," Ricki said repeatedly, trying to calm Kevin down.

"Are you sure? I mean, is everything still attached? Nothing broken?"

"No! I ... Oh, my ..." Ricki turned as white as a sheet.

"What's wrong with you?" Lillian yelled at her, but Ricki didn't answer.

"Come on, say something. What's wrong?" Cathy, too, looked at her, frightened, and Jake thought he was going to faint.

By this time, Carlotta and Brigitte had reached them. Kevin helped his girlfriend to sit up.

"Oh, my ..." whispered Ricki again, her eyes wide open.

"For heaven's sakes, can't you say anything else?" Kevin was scared to death.

Brigitte only now seemed to realize what had happened in the last few minutes and suddenly she could think clearly.

"Ricki, what were you thinking? Are you trying to get yourself killed? I told you –"

"You ... you had your hair cut short," Ricki stammered, staring at her mother.

With a furious look at Kevin and Jake, Brigitte went on.

"And as far as you two are concerned, we're going to have a talk –" Then it hit her. "Say that again," she whispered.

"Your hair ... it's so short."

Gently, Kevin turned Ricki's head toward him. "What color ... is my jacket?" he asked, shaking.

Ricki began to laugh and cry at the same time. "You can see that for yourself, you dummy. You're wearing the red one!"

"You can *see* again!"

"I can't believe it," Jake murmured, touched. He turned away to take the reins of Sharazan and Diablo, who were still standing unattended in the yard – so that no one could see his tears. "Thank you, Lord," he said, head bowed. "You've delivered the miracle I've been praying for."

*

The next day, Ricki came back from the examination at the eye clinic in a fantastic mood.

The doctor felt that it was a pretty safe bet to assume now that his trauma theory was correct, and that the new trauma, of falling out of the saddle and being jolted to the ground, had been the catalyst that brought back Ricki's eyesight. Jake, of course, said that was just mumbo jumbo to explain the miracle he'd been praying for. Of course there would be further tests, but for now, Ricki could still see perfectly.

*

"I'm so happy!" sighed Ricki contentedly, and looked at Kevin as though she were seeing him for the first time. She saw details she had never noticed before her blindness. The slight reddish tone of his otherwise brown eyebrows, the

151

almost invisible scar on his forehead beneath his hairline ... Ricki was getting to know her boyfriend all over again, and beginning to see her world in a completely new light.

But there was another, even more miraculous, gift. Her mother had finally given up trying to talk her out of riding. Brigitte even came to understand that Diablo was the real reason why Ricki could see again.

Joyfully, Ricki grabbed Kevin's hand and ran with him across the courtyard and into the stable, where Lillian and Cathy were already grooming Holli and Rashid.

"Come on, guys. Let's saddle the horses and ride to Echo Lake. I never thought I'd be able to see that wonderful view again."

Lillian looked at her. "Um, that's fine with me, but could we ride past the Western ranch on the way back?" she asked, happiness radiating from her eyes.

"Have you changed your mind about Josh?" Ricki asked with feigned innocence.

"He called last night," Lillian admitted shyly. "We talked for a long time and –"

"And you two are back together again?" Ricki interrupted.

"Yes, and let's just say I hear I have a certain blind friend, and some mistaken dialing, to thank for it!"